ON
THE EDGE

ON THE EDGE

A JOURNEY INTO THE HEART OF CANADA

LINDALEE TRACEY

Douglas & McIntyre
Vancouver / Toronto

Douglas & McIntyre
1615 Venables Street
Vancouver, British Columbia
V5L 2H1

Canadian Cataloguing in Publication Data

Tracey, Lindalee, 1957-
   On the edge

   ISBN 1-55054-126-9

   1. Poor—Canada. 2. Tracey, Lindalee, 1957- —Journeys—Canada.
3. Canada—Description and travel—1981- I. Title.
HC120.P6T73   305.5′69′0971   C93-091595-X

Editing by Lynn Cunningham
Cover design by Rose Cowles
Design by Rose Cowles
Typeset by Vancouver Desktop Publishing Centre
Printed and bound in Canada by Best Gagné Book Manufacturers Inc.
Printed on acid-free paper ∞

"Working Man"—Written by Rita MacNeil
   © 1988, 1993 Paddy's Head Music.
   A Division of Balmur Limited.
   Administrated by *Warner/Chappell Music Canada Ltd.*

Pour Maman, Yolande,
who taught me pride;

Peter,
for bearing the rage and loving so much;

and Liam, my firstborn,
who fills me with hope.

CONTENTS

ACKNOWLEDGEMENTS

The weaknesses of these words and thoughts belong only to me. But whatever good is here has been shaped by the wisdom, skill and friendship of my editor, Lynn Cunningham. I would not have dared this without her. I also extend my gratitude to Scott McIntyre, who believed from the beginning that other voices should be heard and that the country belongs to us all. I thank the Canada Council for its support and guidance, and also the Ontario Arts Council. Whew, my luck held out.

Finally, to those brave and welcoming Canadians who live so invisibly among us: I will forever cherish what you have taught me.

REMEMBERING

The right not to remember belongs to everyone, including those of us who were poor once. In my own family there's argument about our beginnings. Some of us choose to forget, others want to rewrite. We cannot agree on what we were before we became who we are. Fear of judgement guides our memories. It hurts to be poor.

I remember a sweet unknowing before awareness and shame. The cheesy clumps of Kraft Dinner and ketchup in the roof of my mouth. The gummy front-yard tar melting to my shoes in summer. The slow creaking of springs as my mother unfolded her hide-a-bed in the living room each safe night. Gradual awareness made me grow other people's eyes inside my head. Awareness brought shame and a splitting of selves. What I can only understand now is the effort and love that pushed me into myself.

My father was a deadbeat, a man I didn't know. He came and went and left us finally in the dim first months of my life. Years later, he died of cheap drink, unmourned. My mother raised us alone in a disapproving world. She worked as a government clerk and couldn't afford a doctor when she carried me. She got her prenatal care at a free clinic where it was assumed she was unwed, not poor. She heaved me into life at the Salvation Army's Grace Hospital with a doctor she'd never met before. My mother lived for years without her own room, without new clothes, with constant worry that lined her face early. She was poor so her children wouldn't be.

My many people came to this country poor, crowds of them, yelping and hungry, shoved into the sea by the Irish famine, the satanic Yorkshire mills, France's promise of new beginnings. It took some of them centuries to inch out of the muck, generation after generation tugging at their roots, at their masters, at the short leash that strangled them.

Poverty and bad luck were recurring patterns in the heavy weave of small-town, rural Canada, at least until the war years. My grandmother's children grew up hungry, with swollen feet from wearing shoes too small for them. But survival was embroidered with religion, duty, familial and almost tribal allegiances, small decencies and self-esteem. Poverty was gnawing, but the poor belonged somewhere, were good at something. There was shame, there always is, but not the glare of economic disparity, the television-induced hunger and covetousness. Any job was a good job.

My mother's generation moved out of the small towns, still the owners of their language and stories and songs. These were the sounds that wound around their children's hearts, our hearts, words from the mists, from remembered places. The poor moved into the cities, to the edges that were allowed them: clerking, shortorder cooking, the military. Without confidence, without membership. Everything needed to be learned and the learning was done secretly.

These elders of mine believed in fairness, hard work, insisting that they deserved and would reap the rewards of their labour. In time, most of them did.

But the sting of poverty leaves a permanent mark. I look into my family's cupboards and see the excess—the neatly stacked tins of food and cereals. It's a line of defence, a talisman perhaps, against deprivation. When adversity shapes the human heart, the heart is always hungry.

I began, one of the forgetful generation, only inches away from rural poverty, on the western edges of Ottawa. Four small rooms above a diner on Clyde Avenue, a gash of gravel on a hump of clanking industry. People were supposed to work here, not live or raise families. There were no trees, no parks, just the incessant rattle and dark belching of warehouses, factories and rag plants. A place my mother hated.

My brother and I found the grass in the cracks of pavement. We wormed through the tire yards, slid in the sour milk of the dairy grounds, taunted the guard dogs in the greasy guts of the auto-body shop. This was Ottawa's factory belt, bloated each morning with accented workers, Eastern Europeans as I realize now, on the latest immigration wave. They were kind men and women who gave us their empty pop bottles and their friendship, people on their way out, on their way up. I didn't know there *were* other places.

It was the school-bus ride that made me shrink into myself. I saw how other children lived—in real houses, two or three floors high, with backyards and swing sets and new cars. And surely with more perfect parents and clearer hearts than mine. What is it about affluence that gives it the sparkle of moral superiority? That makes its bearers more good and kind and decent? Why are poor people considered so flawed, so failed? I knew this suddenly and completely at age six.

I made a deal with the bus driver: I'd give him peanut-butter sandwiches if he'd pick me up first and drive me home last. Burly, brush-cutted Bob Palen agreed, never asking questions, understanding my secret. For three years we held to this pact—after a couple of months he said he couldn't eat any more sandwiches. Good thing. We couldn't afford to feed him.

All those years on Clyde Avenue, my mother was putting away nickel after nickel. She earned a better job and a bigger salary, enough for a down payment on a bungalow. She did it alone when women weren't supposed to. We moved to suburbia when I was eight. We followed Emily Post's book of etiquette and started using serviettes. My mother grew surer in herself, lighter hearted, and she carried her culture with her, with us—lessons from the poorer places. We lived according to our means, paid with cash, respected authority. We curbed our appetites, made ourselves useful, believing that everything had to be earned. We saved leftovers, coupons and restaurant condiments and recycled long before we loved the planet. We sympathized with the underdog, the bruised, those poorer than us. And my mother bought Canadian so our neighbours wouldn't lose their jobs.

We clung unconsciously to these values. A quiet citizenship, a humble Canadianness. A belief in the rules. It was a simple morality, and as obvious as a cheap suit. I hurried away from these things, forgetting the past and rushing into the future.

That was thirty years ago. Poverty hasn't lessened in this country. We debate how to measure it but not its cause or solutions.

According to Statistics Canada, any family that spends more than 56.2 per cent of its income on food, clothing and shelter is poor. By that measure, over four million Canadians are living in poverty today. The Fraser Institute, the conservative think-tank, defines poverty as the inability to afford the basics. That translates into fewer than a million poor people. It might be more

accurate to say that the institute's approach measures destitu-
tion, not poverty, however, for surely the 2.5 million Canadians
on welfare in 1992 considered themselves poor.

Poverty is defined by what it subtracts from human poten-
tial, and poor people by what they lack. There's slim recognition
of their contribution and social achievements—as taxpayers,
workers, good neighbours, story tellers, cultural guardians,
consumers, parents and volunteers. It's their misery, pitifulness,
victimization that titillate the public, confirming, perhaps, old
assumptions about the defectiveness of the poor. This last year,
editorials and headlines brought many of us to tears over the
million Canadian children living in poverty. But surely if children are hungry, their parents are even hungrier. Where were
the stories about them? Their absence insinuated parental ne-
glect—as if they don't know how to cook or care for their children. The welfare bureaucrats push for nutrition classes while
the poor ask for food, jobs, money.

My wanderings, this book, bring me full circle to myself. To
the Canada I come from. Over seven months I drove across this
roaming geography. Nothing was planned: no prearranged interviews, no schedule. I followed the road and my own random
curiosities. I began my travels with questionable allegiances and
doubts in my heart. I'd grown comfortably distant from my
beginnings, a little romantic about the "Noble Poor." I too carried middle-class suspicions—not so much that the poor create
their own poverty, but that they inadvertently perpetuate it. I
learned differently, painfully, in increments. I came face to face
with the disposable poor: men and women with so few choices
that they live and work invisibly, in danger, in pain.

The poor welcomed me into their kitchens, cars, fields,
slums and trailer homes. I enjoyed Kool-Aid, beer, sometimes a

joint, and we laughed together about their petty indulgences and small larcenies. Often I was honoured with a secret, a private hope, a hidden wound.

I discovered many kinds of poverty, many depths. Some of my new friends had jobs—some had many—others were unemployed, on welfare, retired or retreating into a lifestyle of their own creation. Most of them shared a great personal pride and a remarkable resistance to handouts, preferring their own inventiveness.

I met dirt workers whose cheap labour keeps our fruit prices low, illiterate country people who believe in the value of tending the sick. I worked alongside the women of the Westray mine explosion, shared tea with Vancouver garbage pickers and set up camp with the Montreal homeless. I ate at a soup kitchen with a sickly gay couple and tasted elk with the mother of fifteen native children in Winnipeg. I listened to the memories of an old-age roomer, got drunk with welfare mothers in Cornerbrook and fought back my own pity when I met a disabled woman in Cape Breton. I met old friends whose hard times surprised me and I stumbled on the new poor: the mortgaged suburbanites sneaking to the food bank, the welfare office, the pawnshop.

There were scammers and welfare cheats too, those enemies of the state we so virulently attack in our letters to the editor, but up close their frauds were so pitifully small, they themselves so terrified, that I couldn't hate them. I couldn't even blame them. They lived, like so many poor people, under the weight of their own shame. Such a wearisome thing.

Poverty *is* shameful, but not because decent people fall down on their luck or haven't the resources to act upon what is in their hearts. It's shameful because our economic priorities allow it to exist. My travels have convinced me that poverty is deliberately designed by a nation's greed and complacency. In May 1993 a report prepared by the United Nations Committee on the International Covenant on Economic, Social and Cultural Rights sharply criticized Canada for its growing poverty. It was the harshest attack ever made on an industrialized country.

As I write, more Canadians are unemployed than ever before in our history. The Tory agenda and this new depression have wiped out 1.4 million jobs. A quarter of the manufacturing sector, 500,000 positions, has been obliterated by free trade. The GST, rather than making goods cheaper, has taken $4 billion off the shoulders of corporations and heaped it on to consumers. Who can ignore the glaring inequities? Real-estate moguls can stiff the banks for billions of dollars in loans while a poor single mother in Saskatoon goes to jail for using bad cheques in order to feed her children or a man with AIDS in New Brunswick can't come up with the bus fare to visit the doctor. Perhaps these examples are too morally opaque, the people not fully "deserving." But what of the old and the disabled? I began this journey believing that of all the poor, at least these two groups had won the right to our compassion. Instead, across the country I saw them shoved into the social margins: neglected, lonely, picking garbage from dumpsters.

There is a profound and growing poverty in the land, far deeper than I had imagined. I returned home wondering what distance separates "us" from "them" in these hard times. And who is next?

This is my journey of remembering, my journey to the root of myself, my people, my country. It is an exploration of the keepers of the real spirit of Canada. Beneath poverty's defensiveness, apology and hard exterior of hurt lies a nation's capacity for goodness and rejuvenation. Surely if those on the margins can stay alive in these times, can hold fast to their beliefs and the codes of their lives, can fatten their faith with their own tender mercies, so can the rest of us. For we are, most of us, from this common root. Remember?

THE EAST

Here in the Maritimes, more than anywhere, is the old country—the resource-based economies, the generational poor. There are none of the big industrial cities, fewer of the glaring disparities. The towns and villages offer a sense of community, a softness against the constant hard times, the thud of bad luck, bad health, bad seasons.

Here the country is still human. Still its brother's keeper and good neighbour.

THE ROCK

I've never seen Newfoundland so damned quiet. She's locked in the vice-grip of Easter observances—tense, closed down, her people agonizing with the self-denial of Holy Week. I drive over the balder, eastern side of the Avalon Peninsula, past Brigus South, Admiral's Cove. It's not what I'd hoped. The land flattens into scrubby, treeless tundra. The sky is low and grey, pushing spring back into the ground.

I pull up to a gas station in Cappahayden, into a silent group of raw-looking men. They nod, turning away so as not to cause offence, but watching me anyway. It's the time between times on the Rock, the season of worry and idleness. UI benefits end this month, fishing and government make-work programs have not yet begun. Thirty-five thousand fishermen rely on UI here. A stranger is a welcome diversion.

One of the men sidles over, the ambassador of local curiosities. He's about forty-five, ruddy faced and in overalls.

"Yer travellin' alls alone, are ye?" he inquires, smiling.

"Yep," I reply. His smile broadens.

"Lookin' fer a place, are ye? Not much before Trepassey."

We smile at each other. Cat and mouse.

"Yer welcome to me place. Gotta pull-out couch."

"That's awful nice but . . ."

Mr. Hospitality is grinning now, turning to nod at his companions.

"Lots fer t'eat if ye wants."

My refusal doesn't dim his smile by a single watt.

"No harm to askin', man's gotta try. Right?"

Yep. I push on.

Around me Newfoundland passes. Portugal Cove, Biscay Bay, Trepassey: shuttered, closed-eye settlements kneeling in the scrub. I see no one.

The silence pushes me into myself, into my own unresolved thoughts. What are poor people supposed to be called, I keep wondering. What's proper, inoffensive? People on fixed incomes, low incomes? Underemployed? Down on their luck? But these are apologies, embarrassments.

Even my preferred word is loaded. "Hi, I'm writing a book on poor people." (Oh, you mean *losers*.)

"Poor" is the term I think with; my word for myself, my family. It's my word to reclaim, just as "nigger" is among blacks or "fag" among gays. They're names we've taken back from the dirty mouths of our enemies.

But the poor are as different from each other as anybody else. Some would rather eat their tongues than call themselves poor. And so there are other words. Subtle terms concealing subtle attitudes. A hierarchy of slander. Felt as much as heard.

"Fixed income": Both negative and positive. Used generally for the more "deserving" poor—the elderly, the disabled, abused wives, the middle-class unemployed who are on partial or temporary assistance. Negative meaning: Pensioners should stop whining because they've never had it so good. Positive meaning: Don't give in, don't give up. You're still one of us. You'll be back soon.

"Low income": This is entering the cautiously pejorative. Includes the generational poor, the housing-project poor, single mothers. This is the group most likely to organize and raise hell. They're loathed and feared by welfare bureaucrats. Occasionally they're sacred liberal cows, as in: "I'd like to pay my respects to the human worth of your low income-ness. Can you get your people to put up my election flyers?" The low-income person is often the one in the Bi-Way store haranguing the cashier for a reduced price on damaged kid's wear. Meaning: Overweight, outspoken, angry, unpredictable and always complaining.

"Underemployed": This is a nice one—just mildly reprimanding. Meaning: With a bit more ambition you could work full time. Used often to describe Newfoundland fishermen.

THE BYES OF ST. SHOTTS

There are few clues of life along the desolate Highway 10. Just a stillness and a slow unfreezing. And then the women appear, two and three at a time, walking briskly along the side of the road, red faced and stern against the wind. Out for some air.

St. Shotts stands stiffly on the sky-high cliff of a tiny cove, a silent settlement of a few dozen clapboard houses. There's no one in the yards, on the porches, not even children. I follow the gravel road up the hill to the lighthouse, coming upon a strange sight: three cars parked side by side, blocking my way. I inch past, watching as much as being watched by the dozen men talking to each other through the car windows.

I reach the top, by the shredded mesh of the baseball diamond, park my car and wait out their curiosity. Sure enough, within minutes the procession of battered land yachts crawls by. They turn and park in front of me, eyes glued to their rearviews. Tired of this vehicular mating ritual, I go to them.

"Care fer a smoke?" asks the driver matter-of-factly, as though they'd been waiting for me all day. His name is Eugene, and he's a thick, dark-haired man with a beard and a hungover humour. "How 'bout a beer?" offers John, the thin, freckled man beside him. "Come on in if yer figuring on stayin' alive."

I get into the smoky back seat, a make-shift bar for the barless men of St. Shotts, wondering why they don't do their talking at home with their feet up. "Sure to God we did that last night. We comes here so's de womin won't count 'ow many we've had," Eugene explains.

These are fish-plant workers and fishermen in their middle twenties, taking up where their fathers left off. All unemployed and on UI. "Dem's de lazy man's wages," they cackle, trying to measure my reaction. "And tell us when we'z talking too fast fer ye."

John has an unmistakable authority. He's the travelled man among them, the one who went away to work in a Mississauga factory, one of the thousands of Newfoundlanders who have moved off the Rock looking for employment in the last forty years. But John came back. "Couldn't take de pace," he explains. "It's no life."

Returning home gave John clout. He regales the men with tales of Toronto parking-lot fees as high as the price of a local dinner out, the beggars sleeping on sidewalks, the skinheads at the Eaton Centre, and how there are whole parts of the city where English isn't spoken at all. These are tales as foreign as the Arabian Nights. Through their idle hours the men suck in their breath and whistle low at the strange sophistication of Ontario. They're glad for the stories but even more glad to reclaim one of their own.

But going away made John more self-conscious than the others, more aware of himself and his circumstances. "I guess yous tinking we'z some poor," he ventures. "But here's different from Ontario. We gots our own homes, cars, and we owns our land."

Ownership's an important psychological anchor and a fact that eases the poverty here—almost 80 per cent of Newfoundlanders own their own homes, while the national average is just over 60 per cent. And there's an obvious absence of economic disparity, too. The impossible doesn't stare them in the face.

"Each of dem places about $20,000," John boasts, his hand sweeping across the settlement. "When we need help we gots our friends, de families come out to build or haul, providin' dere's a case a beer to be had." Nods and laughter.

"And we gets our own food mostly," the man beside me says timidly. "Fish, sea birds, gardens, caribou." Joey, a moist-eyed man of twenty-five, slouches shyly in the back seat with me, picking at his beer label, a little dazzled that I'm from away.

"And we don't worry too much about licences neither,"

Eugene grins. "Caribou season's open all year fer us." Another round of laughter.

"We gots our boats, but dere's nothing in dat sea like when our fadders were in it," Joey mumbles. "We'z at de fish plant in Trepassey, waitin' like everyone else for who's gonna buy de place."

"De winter's right long, but we makes our own fun," Eugene bellows, pulling another beer up from the floor.

"Any of you married?" I inquire.

"No."

"Got kids?" There's a grinning silence. Eugene plunges in first.

"He got one," pointing to John. "Me too. It's not like before. Sure me mudder tinks it's bad but de priest christened m'girl right dere in de church. A good party dat was. It's not like before. It's just not shockin'."

The men guzzle the remaining beer. It was nice havin' me over, they say as a way of good-bye. They have to rush off for five o'clock mass, nervous about getting back late and catchin' hell from the women.

JERSEYSIDE: THE SQUATTERS

Three men stumble into the old cemetery over Placentia Bay, coats open and plaid shirts flapping in the wind. They argue and trip over each other in an earnest slapstick as they yank the weeds from a grave. It's a bracing Easter Monday, a time of personal accounting. But the men are not the least bit bound by the sombreness of the place.

The two older men are brothers: Mike is soft and pastel-shaded in a knit sweater and retirement sneakers, Peter is bigger

Left to right: Gerard, Peter and Mike

and baggier in stained denims and rubber boots. He talks excitedly, with a boozy good nature. The younger man, Gerard, is Peter's son. Long and quiet, he's kneeling in the dirt, his old pants riding low.

The men are deciding where to place the new plastic flowers. Peter does most of the out-loud calculations, Gerard the work.

"Me mudder died when I'z out'n de CN boat. Waz a cook," Peter tells me right out. "Never buried her. I comes ta make it right." The woman's been dead twenty years but Peter cries freely, grandly, exercising his emotions while the other two wait. Then the light of an idea spreads across his face. "Let's take missus to the Sea Hall."

It's only just past noon when I'm led like a prize through the dark innards of the Star of the Sea Hall. "Look what we found in the graveyard, byes!" Peter roars. Mike drinks rum and Peter splashes back three beers in the time I have half a pint. Gerard drinks only Coke. No one smokes but me. "It'll kill ya," Peter cautions.

The family tells me about the broken promises of the place: the phosphorus mine that closed two years ago, the GST and 12 per cent provincial sales tax scaring off the tourists, the American base at Argentia that is cutting back on civilian jobs.

"Usta give werk ta 16,000 in de war," Peter spits. "Livin' off er land, marrin' er womin, leavin' dem wit babies. Givin' not a damned ting back."

"Dere's not much on de go fer any us," Gerard mumbles.

"It's yer new Depression, fer sure," Peter agrees. "Harder on de young uns, but still no 'scuse fer a man not t'work." He looks at Gerard, who sinks deeper in his chair. It's an old argument between father and son, a wound deep enough for a stranger to feel.

Gerard is at trade school taking mechanics. It's an unemployment training program. Peter worked all his life. "We workt hard and all's we knowed werz slave wages," he says. Back in his family's growing years he made $250 a month for a wife and nine children.

"But we gots our pension now, byes," Mike chuckles.

"Yer right dere, bye." Peter is sixty-nine. He's robust and in a hurry to grab back all the life the early years took away. "Now let's take ya 'ome, meet de family," he booms.

From the road their home is a plain white clapboard bungalow. It's far back, almost obscured by the newer homes of the grown-up children.

"Come'n see dis, missus," Gerard mumbles. "Wait'll ya see

de back." I'm led by this shy, proud man into the last century. Behind the house is a hill of land you can't see from the road and that's not supposed to exist at all. It's Crown land, illegally farmed, with fences and fields planted right into it. The land's been hand cleared, picked clean by Peter and his boys, then filled with sheep and cows.

The family are squatters, farming land they've neither bought nor paid tax on, winking and grinning about their windfall. None of it's cash crop. It's all survival, food that kept them alive in the lean years, land that kept their self-esteem intact and their need to work satisfied when there was not much else. With the hard times back and their children's children just next door, the work continues and the food is shared.

"We gots babies in 'ere if ya wants a picature," Gerard says. I manoeuvre through the lines of laundry, the woodpiles, the many wandering babies and grandchildren, puzzled by his sudden gregariousness.

The small shed is dark and straw scented. I watch Gerard bottle-feed a newborn lamb, holding it still with a tenderness that surprises me. He's confident here, not timid or tongue-tied, no longer diminished by my city wits or his father's long shadow.

"Almost everting we eats we raises erselves. I'll take ye up to see." Gerard shows me the farm: the sheep, cows and duck pond, the eight chickens and four rabbits. There's a well and cold cellar his father clawed out of the rock, and sheds for wood and hay. There's cod, too: gutted, slapped with salt and spread out stiff like sets of wings.

The farm was all Peter's work at one time, until the boys grew big enough hands to help out. Now it's Gerard who watches over things. "Ain't it someting," he muses, so complete and easy in his pride.

Yes, it is. But it's still his father's handout, his father's land. At least it feels that way.

"Now I wants ye te meet de wife," Peter breathes into my face. He leads me through the back of the house, into the dark kitchen and the darker eyes of "de missus."

At fifty-eight, Anne is tired and silent. Her eyes are ringed with permanent circles, her body soft and caved in with work and the lack of sunshine. I've seen poor wives like Anne all over Canada: quietly competent, unacknowledged, hardened by the worry and fatigue. Not an ounce of spit left over, not even for play.

Anne doesn't rejoice in my sudden company. Instead, she pats her grey hair self-consciously as if that might help put things right. She watches Peter, knowing after thirty-seven years of marriage to see trouble in his gaiety. But hers is a decorous nature, bound by the laws of her upbringing. She puts a plate in front of me: salt beef, turkey, homemade bread and banana loaf. And of course lots of tea. Then Anne folds herself into a chair and closes off.

The kitchen is her domain, a room of memory and of private and public accounting. The men and boys feel foreign in here, cautious. They cross their legs and fold their arms against their chests, hiding their hearts from discovery, afraid of her quiet intelligence. But Gerard is different, easier with his mother, attentive. Siding with her against his father. Another wedge between father and son.

It takes hours for Anne's face to soften to me, for her to be convinced in some secret wordless way that I haven't come to ridicule her man or her home. Nor will her customs allow her to ask a favour of a stranger. She whispers to a daughter, who then relays to me a gentle request not to put Anne's picture in my book. She doesn't want to share her worn face and work dress with the world.

Peter cashes in on my visit to drink too much. He becomes incoherent and his children scatter slowly, fed up with his mutterings. Gerard becomes darker and brooding, ashamed of his father's drinking, ashamed of his own silence and dependence. He'd like his father's approval but there's not much chance of that without a job. Gerard's not moved into his manhood sufficiently to stare down the old man, but I can sense that day is nearing.

Anne stays put on her kitchen chair, quiet, bound by politeness. There's trouble coming: not Peter—they're all used to him. It's the lack of jobs, the UI running out for the younger ones. The farm will put food on their table, give them all a little work. But the younger ones have bigger appetites than their parents. Cable TV, too. Gerard writes to me later in the summer.

"My unemployment is ran out and I can't find a job anywhere. I want to save some money and move away because there's nothing here. Pray for me to get a job. Please. Your friend, Gerard."

DEEP BAY: CURSE OF THE EMPTY SEA

Fogo Island is a lump of rock off the northeast coast. It's where West Countrymen settled three centuries ago with their old King's English. Their 5000 descendants are mostly inshore fishermen, isolated by water and their desire to be left alone.

I wander the island's gravel roads into Deep Bay. Candy-coloured homes exhale wood smoke and frozen laundry hangs on clotheslines. Winter holds everyone hostage; the Atlantic won't move, won't open up. The thaw didn't come until

Carl   Malcolm

mid-June last year. Hardly enough fishing weeks left to qualify
for UI.

Down by the Co-op a couple of men in identical green
overalls work their dory. Carl and his uncle Malcolm prepare
her in the raw wind, ten feet above me. They're confident,
open-faced men, bright-eyed, wind-burned, with a worn wit
between them. As I approach, Malcolm stands up in the same
way his father and grandfather surely did when greeting
women.

"Ye all d'ways from Tore-on-to?" Malcolm asks with genuine surprise. He's the shyer of the two, dark and moustached.
Carl glances at me but stays bent over his work, smirky in his
aviator cap and crooked smile.

"You're the ones wot gave we Brian."

Uhhhh, no. That was Quebec.

"Still gots your crime and murders?"

Uh huh.

"Well, ye don't 'ave to lock 'er up here, missus."

"Are ya sure, with my good looks?"

Carl smiles and lifts his head. "Would ye likes Oi'll show ye de store den," he offers, jumping from the boat. Uncle Malcolm follows behind.

I have passed the pole-up-the-arse test.

Pole-up-the-arse is a popular game with poor people. It's a way to measure a stranger's credentials. The rules are simple: you heap abuse on the newcomer, always disguised as humour, and watch the reaction. People with no sense of humour, who take offence easily or pretend to be deaf, suffer from acute pole-up-the-arse. They're usually self-important: cops, social workers, bailiffs, school principals. And good riddance.

My nose tightens with the stink of tar, wet wool and wood. The "store" is a small equipment shed, dark and closed in. A place to stay clear of the women, to pretend to be busy, especially in the long idle hours of winter.

Here are the cod traps: three-hundred-foot-long square nets rigged with weights to keep them sunk. In another pile are the smaller-weave capelin nets. Every bit of gear, every inch of fishing line, marks the beginning and end of possibility and human effort. Malcolm and Carl hold these things and remember the good and bad years. There have been more bad. But there's no shame among neighbours—an empty sea is a curse to all.

"Oi been fishin' 'alf m'loife, fi'teen years," Carl says deliberately, crouched on the nets. "In dat toime Oi seen de cod catch drop from twelve-tousand-poun hauls a deye t'about four 'undret poinds last year."

In his aviator cap, Carl looks like a World War II pilot fidgeting on the night before death. And it is a kind of death Carl's talking about, the very end of a living, of a way of life. Both men know it and stare silently into themselves for a minute.

Carl made $2500 fishing last year. You'd almost think he wasn't trying. But as he explains, I can see the square hands bleeding on the cod traps, back and arms aching, eyes squinting into the foam for the shrinking fish, and the dull emptiness in the guts when the work is done and the boat is still empty.

Malcolm smokes his last rollie, crushing the butt on the lip of the old wood stove. He grabs a length of rope and twists it awkwardly. "Tis a race 'gainst toime for de summer comes short fer we 'ere," Malcolm shrugs.

Like the fish they catch, Carl and Malcolm are caught in their own net: unemployment insurance, with its changing rules and holes big enough for a man to fall through.

A fisherman's got to work ten weeks to qualify for UI. His benefits are calculated at 60 per cent of his earnings. If he can get in fifteen or more weeks of fishing, he can pick the ten best weeks to average his UI cheques on. So the men work as hard as hell, against the weather, to bring in a good haul. Otherwise they'll starve in the winter. Anyone who doesn't believe UI is an incentive for fishermen doesn't understand human nature.

Whatever few catches they do make give their wives the fish-plant jobs. The women work the Co-op, cleaning, gutting, freezing the cod and sending it off to Boston. Fifty thousand people depend on the fisheries for work in Newfoundland.

"He wot fishes makes werk fer we udders," Malcolm insists.

"And de man wot picks rocks is givin' back nuttin'," Carl rhymes off as mechanically as if he were saying a catechism.

I tag along to Carl's house for lunch. His widowed mother-in-law lives here, useful, grandmotherly, feeding us and the children. Then she curls into the couch and watches "de stories" on TV. The two men drink their beers and eat their meals with the children on their knees.

"Acchhh, but fer all a'we'z complaining, none a'we would leave dis here oiland," Carl says. "It's 'ome, all's we know."

"Some's gone away up along, and sorry for t'go," Malcolm confides, as he tickles his daughter Holly. "We knows dere's no coming back if we goes. So's better for we to be poor 'ere on our oisland than to be poors away."

Not even Joey Smallwood and his call to "Burn yer boats, byes" could chase the Fogo Islanders away from their sea. It's a fact all the oilanders share pride and credit in. Even the ones like Carl who weren't born yet.

"Joey never pulled we off dis rock. Troied some," he chuckles. "Don't expect dese toimes will neither."

Malcolm nods in agreement, looking up from the colouring book he's helping his boy Riley with. "We gots none of yer crime. My girl and boy plays 'ere on dese streets, wit nuttin' fer to torment 'em. We owns our scattered tings, our rigs and gear. Dem homes belong to we, not oweing for nuttin'."

"Floated dem across from Nippards Oiland when Joey made we to smash er boats," Carl explains, waving Holly's crayon. "Somes took de money and settled only dis far. We gots our birds and puffins and caribou . . ."

"Y'ever seen dat, missus?" Malcolm cuts in. "Dey flew dem 'ere fer to feed us."

"Dey takes away our rigs if we's caught poachin'," Carl continues, "but we pays a'mind to whos a'looking. We's doing good even wit de scattered cod. We owes no man."

As the men talk the children wind around their fathers' legs, hold an arm, touch as they're passing. They're not clingy or neurotic. Their bodies are part of the bigger body of their families. And their affections are encouraged and returned by their fathers. It's unselfconscious and sensual, completely loving. It's not the men's faces I watch as much as their fingertips and arms snaking around their children. Making contact. Malcolm and Carl remind me of the fathers I've met in Third World countries. Their ease comes from a lack of alienation, an emotional connectedness, a fearlessness of intimacy. It's one of the most wonderful qualities of real masculinity. Their children grow differently with this love—more considerate, more sure, more contributing, more respectful of women. It's so natural for these two Fogo Island fishermen to love their children like this that they will wonder over these words when they read them.

"D'missus' is makin' a fuss fer wot?" they'll say.

GRAND FALLS: SLIM PICKINGS

The Newfoundland countryside is crowded with "Highways" and "Winter Works" men. There's nowhere to have a discreet roadside pee. I've tried twice and been scared off. For two weeks now I've watched the bush fires burning across the island—white smoke billowing and male faces peeking out suspiciously. This is the kind of work proud men avoid—jobs of last resort for fishermen who can't get enough weeks in to qualify for UI. It's ten weeks of bush and highway work, soul deadening and largely useless.

I stop finally to talk with the very reluctant Mr. Payne. He won't look at me and he won't budge from his heap of burning trees. So I stand in the smoke and peer into his reticence. He will not tell me his first name.

Mr. Payne is a stiff man of thirty, long-faced, with missing front teeth and deep worry lines cut into his forehead.

Intelligent but wounded. He's ashamed of the work he has to do. And I'm the witness. He wants me to leave. I stare through his shame to the man inside.

He finally accepts that I won't go away and slowly unfreezes. He tells me he used to be a lumber man. He used to cut down pine and fir. "Usta werk tirty weeks a'year too." But he says the recycling craze—from the same Central Canadians who shut down the sealing—has broken the back of pulp and paper. There may be other reasons too, but the industry slump has cost 50,000 jobs, and another 150,000 indirectly. Now Mr. Payne's cutting and burning brush in a ten-metre-wide swath beside the highway, clearing the land for fibre optics. It's as menial as yard work, calling on none of his expertise. His buddies are doing the same thing at three-kilometre intervals along the road.

"Tought it sounded good—$600 a kilometre."

But that's all a determined man can do in a week. And when this work's done there will be nothing except more UI, and maybe leaving.

Mr. Payne's gone away from his home for work before, lumbering in northern Alberta. He knows people in the rest of the country think Newfies are lazy. "Shor dere's people dat takes advantage, you can't invent humanity. But I wants to work."

It's Premier Clyde Wells who took his chances away, he says. " 'E promised in d'election to bring every mudder's son 'ome. We got no watchayacall population base. We gots natural resources and nuttin' to do wit 'em now. Who's gonna pull it oudda d'ground and where we gonna sell it?"

I start to lose Mr. Payne after that. But before he closes off completely, I ask him about his wife. He bristles. Mrs. Payne works in a fish plant.

"If I had m'way, no wife 'a mine would 'ave te werk," he

snaps angrily. And with that Mr. Payne ignores me and goes back to dragging trees into the flames.

CORNERBROOK: A NIGHT OUT

"We'se on dick patrol, dat's wot we needs," Cathy bellows in the dark guts of the Padernic Lounge. "Don't cares if I suck 'em er fuck 'em, I gots to have one!"

I have to laugh. And cringe. All of poverty's faces, the stereotypes, are out for a night at the Padernic. There are welfare mothers, bruised divorcees, biker chicks and prostitutes. These are definitely broads—mostly middle-aged, in low-cut dresses and halter tops. They sit in groups swearing loudly, stroking their necks, legs, chests in practiced coyness. Like a bed full of cats.

The Padernic's a moral frontier, a place of subtle but rigid rules. A misstep could land a beer bottle in my face. Everyone carries her own big stick, big mouth, big story. A good yarn can buy you a beer—maybe even a tall pink drink with an umbrella. So they're laid on thick: desperate, funny, tragic tales serialized over many Friday nights and reeled out for the men to bite at. Sailors are the big prize here: it's Norwegians this week. Already made an appearance last night and the women's hopes are running high. The local men are remarkably indistinguishable from one another, sulky and silent, wallets really, lined up three deep at the bar.

Everyone's buying or trading in the Padernic. Except perhaps Jimmy's wife, who just tags after the old man. Jimmy's here in his white shoes every night, smelling of cologne and taking his dancing pleasures with the women. "I only dances," he tells me ruefully. "It's not likes I'z playin' de young games like yous."

"Ten fer forty-two," Mary tells me, screaming over the country band's loud mistakes. She and her friend Cathy have been growing bored with the poor show of men and invite me over. "Ten weeks werk fer forty-two weeksa UI," Mary yells again. "I werks de graveyard, diggin'."

Mary's a short, overweight woman of thirty-nine, the mother of three teen-agers. Her eyes are close-set, making her face hungry and pinched, but her smile is warm and generous. Cathy's her opposite: brooding, angry, a girl of twenty not settled into herself. She sprawls defiantly on the chair and table, a heap of black leather and curses.

"Wot's te do? Pulp 'n' paper 'n dat's fookin' it. I'm on welfare wit me kid."

Where's he now? I ask.

"Wit m'fadder. *Her* ex-husband," she says, nodding at Mary.

"So you're mother and daughter?"

"No." Mary's been married three times. "De second one I divorced 'n married his twin brudder. How's dat fer different?"

"An' dats me fadder," Cathy pipes up. "Fookin' sterange, ain't it? An' he's a bastard." They both agree on that.

I get the next round of Black Horse for Mary and me. Cathy only drinks Coke. "I likes draw." Draw? "Grass. Can't drink beer." A second later Cathy's face contorts in disgust.

"Dat dere's a fookin' pig," Cathy hisses and we all look around. A tall blonde woman drunkenly chases a man through the bar. I don't notice anything until her jacket flaps open, revealing a very pregnant belly. "Dat ain't right," Mary agrees.

It's important to have someone to look down on in a place like this. Suddenly, from behind, a husky voice booms, "Chew me if ya knew me an' blow me if ya know me."

"Ye fookin' slut, get over 'ere," Cathy howls.

"Dey calls er Lady Di," Mary whispers to me, as a thin, brittle woman makes her way to our table.

Lady Di is tough, tight, territorial. I can feel her radar taking every detail of the place into her body, her plan. She looks right through me intentionally. Her thin lips are dangerous. She's an operator, part pro, part giving it away for free. She's making the rounds, a kind of royal walkabout in red high heels and a hard, hurt face, slapping friends, drinking their beer, approaching the line of men at the bar with an almost masculine swagger that pushes them all back a step. It's a beefed-up, raw horniness, rehearsed and defensive. Full of a fear I don't understand yet.

She sits down with us, acknowledging me finally by taking my matches and picking her teeth with them. "Y'ear 'bout de bye could keep it up all night?" she demands. "He weren't no Newfie. Ha!"

Mary has to mull this over a minute before breaking into laughter. "Dat's what we needs!" Cathy hoots, pulling herself up in the chair. "And not one a dem needle dicks," Mary insists. "We wants horse dick. Or one can stay up half de night."

Lady Di decides to park at our table for a while. She leans back in her chair, legs spread open, pelvis out. She undresses the room, the souls of the men, locking finally on a couple of fellows at the bar.

Mary and Cathy watch the room too, but with less hope and certainty. Hard luck is written all over them—something in the tension of the face's muscles, a holding in of the mouth, a withholding of emotion. A hard caution. The beer and the joints relax them, allow their stories out. It's mostly single mother talk:

their kids' colds, the cost of clothes, how expensive it is to find two- and three-bedroom apartments. There's no self-pity—the worry and penny counting are just part of motherhood. And part of motherhood is poverty.

Sixty per cent of single mothers are poor in Canada, mostly because their marriages fail. It's an obscene and avoidable poverty—almost half of separated fathers are in arrears on their child support payments, and a third skip out entirely. "Fookin' dickheads is all they are," Cathy shrugs.

Mary's got a merry-go-round of jobs to provide for her kids: packing and shipping at the Save Easy and Woolco, Winter Works at the graveyard, plus the UI tickets. And once in a while, when nothing else comes through, there's welfare. But that's like being on probation. Welfare's always got their damned snoops paying a visit, looking for men's shoes and extra toothbrushes.

"Dey calls us whores if we gives it fer free," Di cuts in. "Dem welfare inspectors wants every guy we fucks to adopt er kids an' pay er rent. So wot's more de whore?"

"Or dey'll take yer kids. Treatenin' all d'time," Cathy mumbles from a wound deep down.

"Dey comes ta bingo and in de bars watchin' us like we're spendin' dere personal money. A woman dat's enjoying 'erself dey calls unfit. An' a man dat's enjoying 'imself is a hard-working man relaxin'."

"Mosta de women here gots kids an' are tryin'," Mary says softly. "It's nuttin' to no one if they'z out fer a night. Dere back in de mornin' peelin' dere carrots." The women nod in agreement and Lady Di raises her beer as much to us as the two men at the bar.

"An' we'z addin' to d'local economy, parkin' our arses here." We hoot and laugh and then Di skips away to the bar, breaking in on the men's conversation. She knows one of them, but her body goes to work on his friend, arms wrapping around his neck, hips rocking. She hurries back and hauls Cathy to her feet.

"We'z got some draw, let's go," Lady Di whispers, dragging Cathy to the bathroom for a few minutes.

Mary seems so much softer away from the others. So much more vulnerable. She tells me about Charlie, a boy almost, much younger than she.

"He'z gotta big wide dick an' nuttin' upstairs," she smiles. And then a sadness creeps into her face. "He's good fer a visit but not fer a lifetime."

Chances are wearing thin as the night drags on. The men at the bar are finding their courage, trading dances for beers with the thinner women. No one approaches us. Mary turns wistful. Cathy mutters profanities to herself. Lady Di races to our table.

"I gots 'im," she boasts. "From St. John's!"

Then she drags the fellow to the floor and dances too desperately and holds on too tightly. He looks discreetly at his watch. We all wince. And then he tries to bolt. Lady Di pulls him back, suddenly vulnerable, clingy. We can't hear, we can only watch. He pulls away, she pulls him back, she pleads, he gives her a kiss on the cheek. She lets go, almost pushing him.

"De friggin' bastard." Lady Di returns to our safety, defeated. "Said he'z gotta pick up 'is girlfrien' at de bus terminal. 'But I gots an hour left t'be with you,' " she mimics his reply. "Fuck 'im," she howls, looking around the room for another warm body.

The Norwegians don't show up. The night fizzles out with too many unheard stories, too many women sniping at each other, unhaloed by male admiration.

Cathy is stoned and as quiet as the dead. Lady Di is back at the bar, laughing desperately at a wrong man's joke. Mary wants a souvenir. "Ye gots to leave me sometin' to remember ye." It's a command. I go into my car and pull out some talcum powder.

She's the only one of our crowd to leave with something tonight. A small comfort to return to her kitchen with. Tomorrow morning she'll be up early boiling her salt beef and peeling her carrots, spuds and turnips for the traditional island meal called Jig's dinner. It's her daughter's favourite.

NOVA SCOTIA

Nova Scotia is a secretive place, shrouded in codes and suspicion and silence. Its land is worked over with gaping coal mines and insular settlements. If ghosts live anywhere in Canada, they live here. I drive through this place and can so easily imagine the headless horseman, the ghost woman in gauzy taffeta, wailing for retribution. No doubt they're the ghosts of the poor.

The history of Nova Scotia sits like a stone on the bones of the poor: the miners, the fishermen, the Annapolis Valley fruit workers. Poverty is still a shameful thing to admit to here. It's not just pride and privacy that get in the way. It's fear—of ostracism, of condemnation, of falling prey to the social assistance bureaucracies that eat the poor. The fear is more real in Nova Scotia than almost anywhere else I travelled in Canada. And the root of that fear lies in the punitive welfare system.

Social assistance in Nova Scotia is based on the Elizabethan Poor Laws, which gave each town or municipality sovereignty over its poor. Notions of the "deserving" and "undeserving" poor were encoded into law. The deserving poor—widows and cripples—were to be pitied and given charity (just enough to live on) by the churches. The undeserving—unemployed men, battered wives, unwed mothers and their bastards—were sent to poorhouses to work for food.

Two hundred years later, the old poor laws continue to shape Nova Scotia's social assistance program. Sixty-six different welfare policies exist here. Municipalities allot scarce tax dollars by narrowing definitions of "deserving." It's an insidious way of thinking, one that is pervasive in hard times—we begin to scrutinize the needy, to interrogate, to charge them with deceit and fraud. There is inside me too a suspiciousness— maybe the poor *are* too dependent, too complacent. Am I being conned, swayed, suckered by their sob stories? I don't think so, but a lot of decent Canadians believe all this. There's a need to place blame, to be let off the hook. Traditionally allies, the middle class turns on the poor when its members feel overburdened, afraid of job loss and rising taxes. The hatred finds its way into the op-ed pages, into the headlines and middle-class tax revolts. Neighbours and friends are called welfare bums, and we as a society go backwards in time to the Elizabethan tradition of exiling the poor. Our stinginess and mean-spiritedness extend even to the so-called "deserving" poor.

LITTLE BRAS D'OR: LOVE IN THE DARK

I catch Sophie as stark and raw as if I were seeing her naked. She's a big, soft woman: two hundred pounds of unsunned, goose-white skin. She sits alone in her trailer home, doing nothing. No book. No needlework. Just staring into nothing. I can't imagine what she's imagining but I watch her shamelessly,

Left to right: Sophie, Leo and Jimmy

examining her solitude as if she weren't there at all. I know I won't get caught. To stare at Sophie is to stare down the terror of blindness and a horrible lack of privacy.

Sophie moves her head towards me, looking for shadows. Feeling the weight of my body moving in her home. I touch her hand, hold it to my face. She throws her head back, concentrating with her fingertips. And then she groans.

"Owwwwww, wawawawa."

Sophie is deaf as well as virtually blind. The sound she makes is primal, pushed up from her belly, full of frustration and insistence. Awful.

"Owwww. Wawawawawa."

Worse are her facial contortions. The way her mouth forms a big black O like the mad shrieker in Munch's *The Scream*. Her embarrassing absence of vanity. I don't know what to do. I feel pity. I wonder if I should leave.

It was her brother-in-law, dark, vacant Jimmy, who brought

me here. He'd been walking on the road outside Sydney Mines, freezing, when I stopped to ask directions. I offered him a ride up the road. And he offered me coffee at his brother and sister-in-law's place. Then he left me in the kitchen and went to put on some music.

As Jimmy emerges from the hallway, heavy metal is blasting. What does it matter? Sophie can't hear. She's still grunting and contorting, trying to understand who I am. Jimmy looks at her dismissively. "If I were her, I'da killed myself long ago," he says. Then he pounds his fist on the table to get Sophie's attention. "*She . . . is . . . a . . . writer*," Jimmy screams, pressing his fingers, his clumsy signing, into Sophie's hand. "*A . . . friend.*"

Sophie stops, listens, feels, then retreats into the back of the trailer, to the tiny bedroom she shares with her husband. She returns with an armful of metal-jacketed books, like secret files. They're Braille readers, stamped CNIB. She thinks I'm from the institute for the blind.

Jimmy slams his fist down on the table again. "*No . . . Sophie. She's . . . not . . . a . . . teacher.*" It's no use; Sophie's sure I am. The teachers came last year, three times, when Sophie's eyes were much better. They taught her Braille, left some books and then vanished. They'd run out of funding for their home-visit program. But I find that out later. No one thought to tell Sophie.

Finally, an hour later, she's convinced. But it only leaves a silence between us. Sophie pulls out an old blue Olivetti and types out a list of thoughts, then hands it to me.

"i cant see drk tonight.

"do yo uswimming?

"i i can make chicken and turkey.

"do you want a drink of tea and coffee ?

"do yo u working ?"

It's my turn to respond but Sophie stops me. She pulls back the typewriter and punches out a few more words.

"I cant to see I little see the paper."

Sophie can't see the small typewriter print. And she can barely write. She hands me a black marker and paper, then motions me to print in big letters. I'm not even finished when she snatches my paper and holds it close to her eyes.

"Ahhhhhhh. Eye-ee-ter, eye-ee-ter."

Yes. I'm an eye-ee-ter. A writer. It's a moment of exquisite triumph. We nod and smile and pat each other's hands. And then we hurry into our friendship.

"Do you eating eel and potato?"

Oh God no.

"Can you crochet and knitting?"

No. Can you?

"Ah ah." Yes.

"Ow. Ow." Come. Come.

Sophie waves me into her living room of crocheted doilies, pillow slips, arm covers. The room's blanketed with the stuff. She holds one up and pats her chest. "Mine," she is telling me. "I made this." There's so much pride in her gesture, so much effort and expertise in her work. She sells her crochet for $10 a piece at the local stores. It's the only money she makes herself.

"Ow, ow." Come, come, Sophie howls. She rocks her arms as if holding a baby, and points. The walls and shelves are plastered, shrinelike, with pictures of Mary, her daughter. She leads me through the child's life, knowing by memory what face each picture holds. There's the newborn, the toddler, the little girl, the high-school student. Sophie crows about how well Mary does in school, jabbing my arm, pretending to read and making an okay sign. They're big, brutal gestures but I'm beginning to divine the tendernesses, the subtleties they hold.

When Mary was born the doctors wouldn't let Sophie take her out of the hospital alone. Sophie couldn't hear her cries, wouldn't know when something went wrong. They insisted Sophie's mother-in-law be the baby's legal guardian. There wasn't a choice. The grandmother lives just in front, on the same property. She's taught Mary how to talk. But for fifteen years the family's had to put up with spot checks from Children's Services.

But there's no evidence of that hard luck between Sophie and her husband, Leo. No lasting scar. Leo bursts into the house and they're a flurry of fingertips and body parts, touching, holding, slapping together. He's a short, ruddy, red-haired man. Playful and kind. He and Sophie are still, remarkably, in love.

In a couple of minutes Leo is spinning wildly around the small kitchen, telling me how they used to dance together.

"I anse vast"—I dance fast—he says, pulling at Sophie, who slaps him away. Sophie can't keep up, he says in jest. So he goes alone and dances with all the other girls. He signs this last comment to Sophie who punches him good-naturedly. Leo pulls an imaginary beard teasingly. "I'm just joking," it means in sign.

"Usta anse. Naw now." There's no more money for restaurants and clubs. "Ju chi an op"—just chips and pop. The whole family lives on Leo's disability cheque of $704 a month. Sophie gets nothing because she's never had a job outside the home. Nor is her blindness considered disabling. Not until it's total. More than four million Canadians are disabled. And like Sophie and Leo, they live in some of the deepest poverty in Canada. I find it shocking, disgusting, immensely sad. What the hell has gone wrong? Surely they are the most deserving, the most worthy of a hand up. Didn't we agree on that? Weren't we all persuaded by the big, much-ballyhooed campaign to integrate the disabled, to welcome them into our communities, to deinstitutionalize them? But still they're poor, now locked into more private ghettos.

It wasn't supposed to turn out this way for Leo. He'd carefully plotted his course in life. He'd taken auto mechanics at a trade school for the deaf in Amherst, then worked twenty years at the neighbourhood shop as an auto-body man. Leo had bought this trailer home, his car. Then he'd left to start his own garage—it was a small miracle. Only 40 per cent of the disabled work and, of those, 40 per cent are crammed into manual jobs. But he had to stop working when he got three slipped discs in his back.

Luckily, there's no rent to pay. But there's $200 a month for lights and heat, $350 for food, car payments and insurance and a teen-age daughter who insists on certain necessities. Leo takes care of his wife, his daughter and now his ailing, wheezing mother. His courage and kindness come from his own self-esteem, his belief in his own worth, his love for his wife and family.

Before I leave there's something Sophie wants to show me. She walks into the living room and brings back her wedding picture. She and Leo both smile at their younger, slimmer, better-looking selves of fifteen years ago.

"Ee ad enty-ive ef eepo an un unded a-ers," Leo explains. We had seventy-five deaf people and a hundred others. All the deaf people were on one side of the room and the other side was very, very loud.

They both laugh and Sophie signs something she wants Leo to repeat to me. Leo smiles and pats her hand lovingly. "Marrying my husband was the happiest day of my life."

STELLARTON: WOMEN OF THE DEEPS

Left to right: Pauline, Evelyn and Lorraine

St. Gregory's Church is strangely colourless, black and white like a silent movie, like the whole of Pictou County. I've never seen so much pain in one place. I've never seen three hundred people be so still.

The priest is flat, mechanical, tired—he's buried too many husbands this week. No one can absorb the proportions of the loss. Twenty-six miners are dead. God's word cannot be translated clearly enough for any of us to understand. There's a necessary blankness.

People sit silently in the church pews, straight-backed, like they were taught in school. Humility hides their heroics—a

week full of small mercies and quiet acts of courage. I see the
faces of firemen, draegermen, who hours ago were plumbing
the pit. They sit well scrubbed and unblinking. And then there
are the matrons, the mothers, the girls—modest and almost
invisible. It was these women, above ground, who did the worst
work: the mending of hearts. They sustained a remarkable
steadiness through the hurt and chores and sandwich-making.
Through the holding up of widows in their caved-in world.

Evelyn brushes my hand and slips into the pew ahead of
me. It's the first time I've seen her in a dress. She's a little
high-strung today, a little afraid. She hates funerals. But she had
to come to this one. We all did.

It was Evelyn who started the emergency day care for the
families, Evelyn, the unlikely, unassuming leader who circumstances spit up. It wasn't the easiest time in her life to be generous—the recent separation had been messy, the part-time
babysitting and the UI cheques were barely enough for her and
the three boys.

Life here, as Evelyn's learned it, is the art of bending to fate:
bad marriages, parsimonious mine owners, acts of God, are all
cursed and somehow lived with. What keeps hearts from dark-
ening is the delicate embroidery of small decencies, good manners and a rigid propriety. It's a cloying thing for anyone from
away. Even Evelyn's thought of leaving, but she got only as far
as across the street. Where else is there to get to? This is her
place, these are her people; their every birth, death, wayward
son, laid-off husband and family quarrel is a part of her body, a
claim on her heart.

When her phone rang with news about the Westray explosion, Evelyn raced to an Anglican church, as certain of her plan
as she was of her place. I'd been driving right into the headlines
when I heard about her work and volunteered. A dozen of us

became trench-mates, friends, because, as we found out, the act of waiting and comforting small children is no less horrible than fighting a war. Five or six times a day the children prayed for their fathers. We saw their mothers collapse in grief and we heard a little girl curse like a stevedore when the rescuers couldn't bring her daddy's body up. Now our final act of to-getherness is to honour a man we don't know, a stranger in a mahogany casket. We do it for Vicky and Remi, his wife and son.

Evelyn, Pauline, Paula, Lorraine, Debbie, me, all we day-care women raise our chins in unison. Vicky is coming down the aisle—pale and little and dressed in black. Bent over with polio. She's Cree, almond-eyed and dark. There's pain and fatigue scratched into her face, a whole life's worth. Vicky's deep in shock, unsteady, unseeing. Today she'll bury Ray in Nova Sco-tia. A week ago she'd been cursing him for being late. Vicky thought her husband had been downing a few with the boys. When she called around looking for him, a friend was awk-ward.

"You don't know . . .?"

He put his wife on the phone and in a split second Vicky's heart heaved into darkness.

For six days and nights the children came, the volunteers came, Vicky came to Evelyn's emergency day care. Her face stood out; her sensitivities were unknown and there was a great fear of offending. Evelyn cut through the hesitancy with immediate friendship. Vicky told us she was from Manitoba. "Been here just four months."

Vicky and Ray had figured Nova Scotia was the place to set down roots for themselves and two-year-old Remi. Twelve years they'd been together, chasing down mine work across

Manitoba, Ontario and now Nova Scotia. They were finally getting clear— paid off Visa, but still awful broke. Not even a stove to call their own. Ray said in a few months they'd start buying all that stuff: beds, bureaus, the whole bit.

You could feel the women's hearts break. We took little Remi into our arms and Vicky trudged home alone to wait for news and to steady herself.

The days were lost to the details of children: runny noses, missing toys, fussy eaters. I hadn't been so tired since I gave birth. None of the volunteers slept much. We sat for a week in the twitching circle of lobby light, chain-smoking, guarding the dreams of the miners' children, rocking the frightened ones back to sleep. We were all unwashed and unmade up, kept alive with coffee, doughnuts and adrenalin.

Evelyn ran the place, gently, like her own home—with lists and chores and common sense. And a mother's sense of the possible. The waiting and the work were punctuated with news and rumours of the rescue. We heard that roofs and walls were collapsing, that men were inching like worms through holes no bigger than oil drums. Rescuers had to pick rocks by hand in the dark. We shook our heads among ourselves.

None of the women had time to grumble against the mine owners. There was a need to pull together to get the buried men out. No use blackening hearts or slowing down hands with blame and recrimination. "There'll be time enough for that when the inquiry comes," Evelyn said impatiently. "What's the use of it now when we've got their children to keep going?"

And their wives. Evelyn took Vicky into her heart in the only way she knew how—completely. She'd pieced together Vicky's circumstances by putting her ear to a county-wide network of gossip and half-truths. We knew already that Vicky didn't have a stove. Evelyn worried that she didn't have food or money. She set about cadging favours and handouts that she would never have dared seek for herself. And she called her ally: the sweet, white-haired Mayor Porter. He'd see to it that Vicky got a stove and a cupboard full of food. And she'd never know how.

On Thursday our hearts sank lowest. "The search is off, they've called it off," a woman shrieked. Our work was done. The rest was left to the funeral directors and clergy.

Ray's casket is a dark, rich brown mahogany with brass rings. A family portrait sits on top, along with a moose-skin shirt, the one Vicky's grandmother made him. It's so strange to see a man's entire life abbreviated to these few details.

The priest begins with a simple statement of fact: No one here knew Ray. Vicky is helped to the altar by her family, who've come in from Manitoba. She reads from her notes with a dignity and courage that takes our breath away.

"None of you really knew Ray or that he liked to fish and never caught much. I'll always be grateful for having him for twelve years. Not a day went by that he didn't say he loved me. And every meal I ever cooked for him, he never forgot to thank me. I want to thank you all, I'll never be able to say enough good things about Pictou. Canada's got a lot to learn from the people here. Thanks for taking the time to be here today."

As Vicky follows Ray's body from the church, Evelyn reaches out to touch her hand, breaking with the codes of this place. Ray's body is committed to the ground and Vicky's family join hands, moving in circles around the grave. It's the Cree way—walking the spirit into the next world.

Five days later Evelyn moves Vicky and Remi into her own house when Vicky's grief makes her afraid to stay alone. Evelyn's three sons babysit for Vicky and chase Remi around with the rough male play he so needs now. Secretly, Evelyn worries about food money, milk money, but she says nothing. It would go against her pride and her strict sense of propriety.

I drive sadly away from Evelyn, from Stellarton, along the 106 northward to the P.E.I. ferry in Caribou. It's still just spring here; the smell of cut grass and lilacs surprises me. I feel like I've been here for many seasons, many lifetimes. At the asphalt ferry dock I'm slapped suddenly by Rita MacNeil's Cape Breton voice. I sit in my car and weep.

> It's a working man I am
> And I've been underground
> And I swear to God if I ever see the sun
> Or for any length of time
> I can hold it in my mind
> I never again will go down underground.

PRINCE EDWARD ISLAND

I feel blunted after Westray. Outside myself. I wish Evelyn were here. I miss our usefulness, how the work kept our hearts in one piece. I line up my son and husband's photographs along the ledge of the dash and that helps.

I know Prince Edward Island like a teen-ager knows her lover. Adoringly. With a need for relief. But without much critical thought.

I've been coming to the island every summer for years now. I love her soft land and red earth. Her gingerbread and well-mannered gentility. But I've never seen poverty here, and I've never looked for it. There have always been hedges and fields and the back country to separate islanders from tourists. There have been mini-putt and Anne of Green Gables to distract me. The island holds itself to itself more closely in the tourist season. But this is the month before summer. The real islanders are more conspicuous. And so are the poor.

SATURDAY BARGAINS

I stop in Lower Newtown, on the island's southeast side. There's a crowd and I'm curious. I manoeuvre through the cars and pickups, the old folks and kids, inching my way to the centre of the hub. It feels like a country fair.

The contents of a family's home are spread out on a back lawn, gawked at and bid on as an auctioneer jokes. There's a mobile canteen selling pop and sandwiches in the drive. And a small line of eager buyers snaking into the kitchen to pay for their bargains. Quilts are going for $5, a silver tea service for $26. There are hand saws and tools, old sofas and lamps. Even a child's Lego set. The lawn has a "For Sale" sign stuck into it.

It's a foreclosure. I'll see this right across the country. Bankruptcies, too—a steady increase for eight straight years. In 1992, almost 62,000 Canadians went bankrupt.

CHARLOTTETOWN: A ROGUE'S GALLERY

Lawrence Jimmy won third prize in the Charlottetown "Beautify Your Home Contest" in the landlord and tenant category last year. It came with a certificate and a note from the premier. Lawrence Jimmy wished it had come with cash; he'd have put straight into his poker pot. Nonetheless, it was a summer of great pride.

Lawrence Jimmy

His prize-winning garden is a spray of colour and whimsy in a greyish place. Lawrence Jimmy lives in the corner rooms of a decrepit row house. Pots of fuchsia, geraniums, petunias and impatiens hang out front, flamboyant, frivolous. I knock on the door, mistaking the place for a flower shop.

Fifty-one-year-old Lawrence Jimmy emerges with a beer belly and T-shirt, shaggy as a sheepdog: bushy eyebrows, tousled hair. He makes the merry facial efforts of someone trying to stifle a joke or a fart. Not too far below his surface is an eight-year-old kid. Or a favourite uncle. I like him immediately. But he doesn't sell flowers, he just grows them to jazz up the neighbourhood the way his mother did.

"Usta sell antiques though," he says, as if hoping that will do. "Come in, come in."

Lawrence Jimmy is eager for company and pulls me into his tiny dark house with its stamp-sized living room. There's dust everywhere, and smudged, almost opaque, windows.

"And would you happen to have a smoke, missus?"

Lawrence Jimmy shows me a photo album of his prized antique carriages and flow-blue china. "Couldn't keep it," he shrugs. "Had to let 'em go to pay the bills. I had a cabinet full of the stuff. Even had a complete bathroom set of flow-blue. Water jug, chamber pot. Worth about $17,000. Had to sell cheap. My baby strollers too.

"Almost paid up my rent and lights, though. I'm behind on the cable and telephone. It's my own fault. I'm sentimental. I like to call up my friends long distance."

All this I know about Lawrence Jimmy within the first three minutes of meeting him. He's an unrepentant gabber, luring me in with the island's dusty stories and secrets. He's combed every inch of the province's past for bargains and treasures.

"Ya'ever heard of Holy Dollars?" Lawrence Jimmy enthuses. "Wouldn't mind getting my hands on them. Had a few plugs once.

"Way back when the island needed money they used Spanish coins and put holes in the middle of them. Called 'em Holy Dollars. Used them from 1803 to 1805. When they didn't need them no more they put the coins on a ship and the ship sank and was never found. The plug's worth $1000. And the Holy Dollar's worth ten times that much."

Lawrence Jimmy cranes his neck and scratches his stubble in dreamy thoughtfulness. He can see that coin. And all that money. If only . . .

"Oh, if I had the money I'd be doing what you're doing, driving a car, calling on people here and there. Only a month I ask. Oh!" And he laughs at the impossibility.

Jimmy's a believer in luck. An optimist. He was born that way, but antique collecting increased his faith and his itch. So has gambling. He plays poker and bingo and buys 6-49 lottery tickets, sometimes five at a time. It starts at a dollar a dream.

Lawrence Jimmy has the affable charm and quick wit to wring the good out of any situation. Including his chronic unemployment. He used to work at an optical store making glasses and frames. The shop went out of business two years ago and Lawrence roamed from UI to welfare.

"I don't mind saying so—could use a summer off. I get enough fer what I need; more sitting on my arse, in fact, than I could working. Not to say I don't want to work, but what's the use working miles out of town for $5.50 an hour? I got to pay my transportation and meals out there. I end up with $580 a month and $400 of that goes for my rent. See my point?"

I do. Lawrence Jimmy was making little more than the minimum wage and spending 69 per cent of his take-home pay on rent. Minimum wage keeps people in perpetual poverty—it's an elastic band of misery that goes from a low of $4.75 an hour in P.E.I. and Newfoundland to a high of $6.35 in Ontario, and it represents only 37.1 per cent of what average workers make. Almost a million people earn this wage—they don't live on it, they survive it.

But this is *my* rage. It's not in Lawrence Jimmy's nature to ponder the inequity of poverty. It's no more an obstacle than the walls of his own home. It's just something to be manoeuvred around. His life and heart's delight are friends, strangers, good stories, the community of people he grew up with. A few poker winnings. A friendly handout from Mom.

"She's eighty-five, God bless her. She gives me a little when she can—$70 today. That'll get me into the poker game."

Poker's the weak spot. And the gift horse. Lawrence Jimmy usually hosts the games in his kitchen. It's more than hospitality; he gets five bucks from each player. Tonight he's got six players, no, just a sec . . . another guy's on the phone . . . yes! He's in. Seven guys. That's thirty-five beans along with his mother's seventy. Definitely enough to keep a hand in. "And there's no booze. Tried it but the drunks would start arguing with each other. And I don't care for that."

Lawrence Jimmy pulls a couple of crumpled coupons out of his pocket. Pats them flat on the chair arm. "What day's it today?"

"The nineteenth."

"Whoppers half-price at Burger King today. I got two coupons."

"Okay. And I'll buy the fries and drinks."

Lawrence Jimmy and I get into my car and head for the bargains. All the way he jabbers about the neighbourhood, the old people, the island ghosts.

I envy Lawrence Jimmy's contentment—his circle of friends and full private life. So much like my own beginnings. I miss it. Terribly.

I remember my aunts and uncles and cousins convening around a few beers, a single bowl of chips, arguing, listening, laughing with the surest contentment I'll ever know. Our worth was not measured by what we were, where we worked or how we stood in public life. Our real contribution was made in private, to each other—a few bucks here, a set of hands there, a late-night ear, histories told and retold. We lived our lives in that wonderful relief between the work day's end and the next day's beginning, where humanity flowers.

Lawrence Jimmy reminds me of my own lost wealth.

VOICES

I make my way along the northeast coast to Stanhope, my favourite beach. I'm half expecting to find my son there, to hear his noises and shouts. But the off-season is grey and silent and dreary with memories, not people. There's nothing worse than showing up at a place too early or too late.

My mind registers what my body already knows: a cold seems to have settled in my lungs. I feel a weight in my chest, but no phlegm, no congestion. Odd. It comes with a gnawing kind of dread that there's something wrong at home. I call from a phone booth but everything's fine. There's something awful settling on me. I feel spooked.

MORRELL: THE OTHER ANNE

Anne twists obviously in her broken circuitry on the side of the road, hitchhiking. She arranges and rearranges her grocery bags with intense persistence, muttering to herself. I know Anne from the big city—from the wary stares of *clochardes* in Montreal, the vacant belligerence of Toronto's Queen Street roomers, the pleading, open palms of the homeless on Robson in Vancouver. Now I find her in Charlottetown, in torn navy stretch pants and a tight, safety-pinned shirt: witchy, weathered, missing her bottom teeth. She's completely surprised when I stop. "Where ya going?" I ask.

"Just up the road, up the road," she answers. Sixty-five kilometres up the road, but she forgets to tell me that part.

"My name's Anne, aw, Anne," she says eagerly, holding out her hand.

"I'm Lindalee."

"Good to know ya, Belinda, aw, good to know ya."

Anne cannot remain silent, she can't give in to that other noise, the internal one.

"I bin livin' nineteen years with Leonard. He's got eighteen acres, eighteen. Good to me most of the time, most of the time.

Libby *(left)* and Anne

Sometimes he says he don't love me no more, aw, he says he don't love me. Knocked my teeth out once."

"Why does he beat you?" I ask.

Anne ponders the reasons. "I aw, aw . . . I don't know besides his temper. Got a temper. Got a good mother too. Libby. Gotta meet Libby, gotta meet Libby."

Anne doesn't talk about the hospital or the pills; she's learned from the years of jokes and dirty looks not to. But it leaks out of her in an unguarded moment—something about family sticking her in the Riverside. It was a while back.

Anne hitchhikes everywhere, always has—to the grocery store, the laundromat, the bakery for thirty-eight-cent day-olds. She likes the window rolled down and the wind in her face. She likes the straight long lines, so unlike her own mind's thoughts. And a chat with a stranger—a monologue, really. The hitchhiking's not to get somewhere as much as to get away from someplace.

"I had a baby, aw, aw, sure I did. I wasn't married, not

married. So the welfare took him away. He's twenty-one now and he'll come, he'll come. Sure he'll come to find me. Find me."

Anne heaps these shards of history and selves before me like offerings. "I made $600, aw, $600 pickin' blueberries last year."

"How do you make money to live?" I ask.

"Never enough money, never enough; $200 I get from, aw, from the welfare and I works for the nuns, aw, cleaning for the nuns for pay or favours. And Jimmy brings our meat, aw, Leonard's brother, Leonard's brother."

Near Morrell Anne tells me to turn "that way" off Highway 2. She doesn't know her left from her right. There in a clearing is her little yellow cabin, flimsy as cardboard. "Come in. I got Pepsi and 7-Up. You want some?"

Anne's a little flustered to be bringing home a guest. I guess it doesn't happen often. I'm a little afraid—of Leonard, of her, of her strangeness.

It's the combination of poverty and mental illness that makes Anne so unknowable, so unlovable. A million other Canadians have mental illnesses, and like Anne, many of them are doomed to poverty. So they repulse us. We can't stomach their faces, their mismatched clothes, their drooling. We make them unwelcome. And they fade back into the hell of poverty and mental illness. Into the cracks of city sidewalks.

Anne and Leonard live in three and a half rooms. The living room's all of four feet by six. Behind a curtain are the bedroom and a small bathroom. The whole house is as clean as a church.

Some of the furniture I remember from my own childhood: particle-board dressers disguised with stain and veneer, vinyl and chrome kitchen chairs, an Arborite table, shabby linoleum. The jumbled display of trinkets and souvenirs.

"See my Olympic glasses?" Anne points proudly. They're the gas station kind. Hard to get without a car. Precious.

Anne lingers in her hospitality, offering me ham sandwiches, pop, T-shirts, even a shoe bag. Then she wants me to
drive her over to see Leonard's mother. "Ya gotta meet Libby,
gotta meet Libby. She don't get out much. We could take her to
the cemetery, aw, the cemetery." Anne visits Libby once or
twice a day, doing her chores and taking her gifts and groceries.

Libby's trailer is behind a stand of poplars and pine. I catch
a glimpse of the boys, Leonard and his twin brother, Jimmy—silent, watchful, ferret-eyed men. They hide out in the woodshed
during my visit, smoking, drinking and blocking wood for their
mother.

Libby is tending her yard. She's a bowed, leathery-faced
woman, more crab than person. Tiny and spindly with lively
blue eyes and a smoker's hack, Libby pulls herself up as straight
as her God allows and waves me into her home. Inside, Anne
hands her a bottle of vodka from a brown paper bag. Libby
pours a snort into a cup and adds water. She's mindful of how
this looks to a stranger. "I takes a bit about once a week. Makes
me feel good. Not to git drunk, mindcha, just to put me in gear."
She swallows it down all in one go.

The inside of Libby French's trailer holds the colourful congestion of a whole life's worth of memories and doodads. There
are swag lamps, glass sets, plastic poinsettias, velvet paintings,
teddy bears, crocheted pillow slips. Sitting on the kitchen table,
apart from the clutter, is an old sepia photograph of a young
man with big ears. Libby's husband.

"That's Papa," Libby rasps, hunched over her tray of to-
bacco. "Died five years ago. Only had $400 saved up. So I'd to
sell the truck for to pay the funeral and burial."

"But it was some lovely, aw, some lovely that funeral. Eh,
Libby. Eh? Show 'er the picture of Frank in his coffin, aw, Frank
in his coffin." Libby nods, handing me the photograph. Sure

enough, there's Papa, very white and very dead, lying on satin. But Libby's not looking. Her eyes go rheumy and turn inward. All she wants is to lie beside Papa.

"You got kids, Belinda, you got kids?" Anne says urgently, worried about Libby slipping away.

I take out my pictures of Liam. "You only got the one?" Libby chides, perking up. "Sugar! I had me eight and me picking potatoes with a belly out to here. Had to. All the young ones with me and all of us working for wages. Girl, am I some sick of them spuds."

As Libby talks, Anne works silently at the wood stove, stirring beans and serving biscuits and glasses of Tang. Libby hardly notices.

"I lived the thirties," Libby tells me. "Born in 1918 and I'm telling you these times are just like them times. All them hungry people aching for food and justice."

"That's right, Libby, that's right." Anne chimes.

"It's going like the Depression. No work. Then no food. My Jimmy's over at the butcher's working for meat, not wages. Fills up my freezer and sends some over to Leonard's place too. I gives him some of what I got from the pension. And that's how it goes."

"Hey, Libby, what's heaven like?" Anne asks guilelessly.

"I rightly don't know. I 'spect it's good. There's gotta be a God, how else's all of it come to us. You puts a seed in the ground and something grows. You gots sky and earth and fish. That's gotta be His hand."

She ponders a moment. "Not everyone gets to go, you know. Don't know if you can fly like angels or not, but it's s'posed to be good."

Anne smiles crookedly at me, pleased that Libby's talking.

The next day when I drop in to say good-bye, Anne hurries

to her room and pulls out a big bargain bag of toilet paper.

"This was some deal, some deal, Belinda. Only $1.83. Have some, aw, have some."

Anne hands me two rolls of toilet paper.

"Can't call me stingy, aw, can't call me stingy."

She's beaming from ear to ear.

A DYING ROOT

After leaving Anne I'm suddenly in a hurry to get off the island—chased off, really, by a sense of apprehension, that damn ache in my lungs and a poisonous kind of adrenalin. I've convinced myself I'm dying of pneumonia.

I boot it to Borden for the ferry. Two hours later, I'm in New Brunswick, frantically heading north into Acadian country. But I'm heading home, led by a strange instinct that is stronger than logic. My heart knows its root is dying.

I drive for hours, watching the sky for night, watching the villages for a phone booth. My lungs are in pain, my mind feverish. Finally, near Richibucto, I find a phone outside a corner store. I call my mother. Her voice is small and wrung out.

It's Gramma. Her lungs are taking in fluid and she's sinking, sinking like a good, great ship into the sea. I try not to cry on the sidewalk, I try to get to my car, but I burst halfway there, sobbing and hurt and embarrassed. Strangers offer me an arm, directions, a way out of this place.

And then I realize . . . the pain in *my* lungs is gone.

In the Ottawa hospital I can smell the dying before I see it— sweet and yeasty, like the smell of birthing. I walk into the hushed, bilingual murmur of my big family, into their bosoms, shoulders, arms and tears.

Gramma looks so old and translucent, so characterless. Her teeth are missing. There's an IV and an oxygen mask over a face I don't know any more. Where's the tough-like-a-boxer, pretentious old Brit? Where's the soft, sad little girl who left her dreams in a Yorkshire mill at the age of twelve? The immigrant who came to French Canada? The mother who bore ten children and raised seven of them in dirt poverty? Gramma is dying more from exhaustion than cancer.

She's not left alone for a single moment. All her children are here, my aunts and uncles. And the grandchildren too. We take up our vigil naturally, two at a time. I partner up with *ma tante* Denise. The others go home to rest, prepare food, make arrangements. No hands are idle, no grief is left to fester.

Gramma can't talk now, nor can she see except perhaps to the depths of her own beginnings. Her eyes are open, unblinking and milky. But I know she can hear me, and I read from Corinthians, not so much because I'm a believer in God as because I'm a believer in love. It's Gramma's favourite passage, the one she read at my wedding. I try to keep my voice steady. A circle is closing.

Gramma was always my favourite relative. I easily forgave her her Baptist indignation, her rigid morality, the conceits and superiority that hid her smallness and fears. She'd acquired an exaggerated Britishness, a kind of aping of the upper classes that some of the family found artificial and grating. I loved it. I suspect it kept her sane.

Gramma had wanted to be a writer, a traveller. Instead she had to go to work in a cotton mill. But she could read and write. She spent years, decades, of a bad marriage in white-knuckled silence and rage. But I knew her much later, when she'd reinvented herself. After poverty and abuse, after the children had grown, Gramma left her husband with one last child in tow. She arrived in Ottawa and scrounged work as a government clerk. That's when she took on her aristocratic airs—collecting her spoons and china teacups and Royal Doulton figurines. These were beautiful things, treasures that I stared at greedily and was forbidden to touch as a young girl. I thought Gramma was a high-born British lady. I learned later she was an imposter, and a bad one at that. Her aristocracy and changing family lineage were a poor woman's romantic invention. What she was was an escapee, a survivor with immense pride, dignity and inventiveness. All her life she carried her past and her poverty like a curse, afraid of being found out, judged, excluded. Behind her own petty bigotry sat a shame as heavy as stone.

It was in retirement that Gramma was finally able to feed her hungers and vanities. The Canada Pension gave her more money, more regularly, than she'd ever had before. It freed her generation from fear and proved that poverty could be eradicated without wounding the middle class. Clutching her bus pass and her senior's ID, Miriam Ainsworth Lalumiere travelled all over the continent, even back to England. She took up theatre and swimming and painted well enough to teach. This is the grey, limp woman who lies before me, at the end of her many lives.

Throughout the last days and nights ma tante Denise and I sing old British songs to comfort Gramma.

"Oranges and lemons / Say the Bells of St. Clement's."
"The Grand Old Duke of York / He had ten thousand men."
"It's a long way to Tipperary / It's a long way to go."
And then the hymns.

One night a small tremulous voice calls from the other side

of the curtain. It's Mrs. MacDonald, a feeble, dying woman who shares the room. "Oh, dear, it's so lovely. Could you sing me the 'Hawaiian Wedding Song'?" I could cry. I don't know the 'Hawaiian Wedding Song.' Where are her people? Why is she so alone? The whole ward is full of old lonely dying people.

Nothing could keep our family away from Gramma in these last years, these last days. It's the way we were brought up, the values that Gramma herself passed on to us. None of the older people in my Lalumiere clan will ever die alone, staring at a hospital ceiling like Mrs. MacDonald. I'm not so sure of my generation. Our affluence has poisoned us a little, hardened our hearts. Pushed us away from ourselves. From each other.

I'm alone with Gramma in the hours before her death. Miriam Lalumiere leaves with a faith in her God and a final lack of shame.

MIRIAM'S MARKINGS

After she's gone, I wander through Gramma's Bibles looking for her. She's made many scribbles and exclamation marks on the pages. The bitter, humourless admonishments of St. Paul are darkly underlined: damn the fornicators and drunks—words of comfort for her many past wounds. But there are other words Miriam has circled.

"For the poor shall never cease out of the land: therefore I command thee, saying, Thou shalt open thine hand wide unto thy brother, to thy poor, and to thy needy, in thy land."—Deuteronomy 15:11.

"For the needy shall not always be forgotten: the expectation of the poor shall not perish forever."—Psalm 9:18.

"For the oppression of the poor, for the sighing of the needy, now will I arise, saith the Lord; I will set him in safety from him that puffeth at him."—Psalm 12:5.

"But ye have despised the poor."—James 2:6.

NEW BRUNSWICK

I return to my travels, carrying my grief into New Brunswick. So much of the province is bush and I wander peacefully at first, enjoying the solitude. But there's a despair here, an aching lack of work. All along the highway I see front yards and porches cluttered with kitchen goods and hardware. These are permanent yard sales, the only way some people have left to make a wage. It's such a naked display. Men and women sit all day beside their teapots and old 78s and car parts, waiting for a sale. I can barely return their hungry looks.

SAINT JOHN: THE WINDOW PEOPLE

Every morning Myles and Syd crawl out of bed to a pot of coffee and a game of crib. They set themselves up at the table by the front window, smoking rollies and watching the street come alive. Southend is the rundown part of Saint John—uneven sidewalks, absentee landlords and broken plumbing. The area's neck-deep in hungry looks, dirty looks, hostile kids and furtive refugee claimants. It feels a lot like the place I lived in as a kid. Locals turn a cold face to people not from here. I stare back at the hate until it changes into something else.

Myles and Syd know everybody's business around here. They spend most of the day in their three dark rooms. There aren't even bus tickets to get across town.

Myles *(left)* and Syd

The window's their cheapest escape, so they watch—the drivers parking illegally, the unmarked police car, the old woman picking butts off the sidewalk. They especially like the old woman.

"Sometimes we give her a little kiss," Syd chuckles.

"Sometimes we seen guys throw change at her like she had no feelings," Myles says. "We go out and help her."

All day long Syd and Myles sit in their window, thinking up odd jobs, putting together jigsaw puzzles, arguing over the last few dollars of their welfare cheque. Then, as regular as clockwork, one picks a fight with the other and some steam gets let out. Today it's crochet. Myles is arranging his hand-made bedspreads and cozies, talking about the old lover who taught him to crochet.

"Oh, which one was that?" Syd inquires snidely.

"You wouldn't know him."

"I've known a lot of guys."

"It's nothing to be proud of."

"It is if you knew how good they were."

Back and forth, maiming each other, and then a bitter silence. They stare out the window. It's the boredom of poverty; there's damned little distraction apart from emotional gymnastics and invented dramas. Their year-old love is nervous, insecure, jealous. But just as often, forgiving and hopeful.

"How's this for an idea?" Syd says cheerfully, trying to lighten the mood. "How's about we sell the crochet at the flea market and you could do live demonstrations?"

"They'll think we're a couple of fags."

"We *are* a couple of fags, Myles," Syd deadpans.

They both laugh.

"And believe me, this isn't Montreal or Toronto," Syd explains to me. "I been to Montreal when guys were holding hands in the street. You'd never see that in Saint John unless one of 'em was dead."

To emphasize his point, Syd rolls up his pant leg and shows me a big red gash. Last spring, just across the street, he got jumped by five teen-age boys with baseball bats. Fag bashers. They beat in his legs, squashing him like a bug on the ground. People on the sidewalk just vanished. Finally someone stepped in and got him to the hospital. "It made me feel sick. Took me months to be able to walk on the street without looking in alleyways and around corners."

Syd's ashamed of his vulnerability, of carrying somebody else's sickness inside him. Myles brushes his hand against Syd's arm, a little fortification.

Syd and Myles's arrival in Southend is as predictable as anyone else's. Syd spent years hustling on the streets. In the end, the game changed and hungrier young boys were doing a lot more for a dollar. At thirty-nine he's more weary and worldly than Myles, not expecting as much, not as easily disappointed.

He's tall and wiry, with a lived-in face. His straight work has been mainly janitorial. "It's all I can really do."

Myles's face is marked with a bruised and frightened boyishness. His childhood was battered by chronic poverty, welfare and alcoholism. He's got no bottom teeth and his nails are bitten down and yellow with nicotine stains. But there's something immensely kind and well mannered about Myles, a goodness his mother gave him despite his father's brutality. He's thirty-six and still sees the world with a child's hope and belief in magic. Sometimes he wanders into a deep and private sadness, staring out the window in mid-conversation. Myles is HIV-positive, has been since 1985. He's on five different medications. His health is fragile and the fear of full-blown AIDS, of dying slowly, piece by piece, freezes his guts every morning when he wakes up.

Myles has got a stack of AIDS pamphlets and booklets. He knows all about his nutritional requirements: milk, meat, fruit and vegetables. But there's no money, no way he can eat like that. He can barely scrape together the bus fare for his doctor's visits from his food budget. It's nickel-and-diming the devil away—collecting pop cans, distributing flyers, selling crochet, anything to augment the $600 a month in welfare.

"I hate myself for getting AIDS," Myles stammers. "I hate myself. It gets in the way all the time." A single tear rolls down his cheek and falls onto his jeans. "I'm sorry," he whispers. Syd pats his hand.

Myles and Syd are socially alone, isolated. They don't belong to the tentative gay scene of Saint John. They don't make it with the fashionable gays, the ones cruising Rockwood Park in their Goretex jogging gear. In fact, taste—that wonderfully bourgeois conceit appropriated by gays as a badge of cultural identity—isn't an obvious attribute in either man. They don't know Mapplethorpe's photographs, Joe Orton's angry theatre. They couldn't tell Baroque from Byzantine. Their culture is polyester: Myles loves the music of the California Raisins, Syd wonders if Elvis is really dead or if someone else was put in his coffin instead. Art is what's on a drugstore calendar. They live their homosexuality privately, with Victorian discretion. The public affirmation of other gays in other places is both repulsive and enticing, requiring a courage and a community they don't have.

But it's not just the narrow attitudes of Saint John that push Syd and Myles into invisibility, it's chronic poverty—reducing them to the skeletal remains of their characters, the fault lines of their psyches, their inevitably flawed humanness. Poverty illuminates, with the harshness of a thousand suns, every inch of fat, every patch of dried skin and bald pate, every drooping buttock, bloated belly, flabby thigh, crossed eye, hollowed, hallowed human face.

Poverty is unforgiving and as obvious as a facial scar. The middle classes can't stomach it. Straight or gay, they're obsessed with appearances, plumage and the culture of permanent youth. Poor gays are despised by their own.

Myles calls those kinds of gays "snobs" and conceals his hurt with contempt. His identity is shaped far more by his own generosity and citizenship. Myles is a volunteer for the Cancer Society and the local AIDS group. For years he worked at Meals on Wheels, but they stopped calling. He thinks it's because he's HIV-positive. Myles performs good deeds as persistently as a boy scout and he's won precious awards for it.

"See: citizen of the week," he points out, holding up his photo album. A news clipping dated April 22, 1986, acknowledges his work for Meals on Wheels. And there's the Saint John Volunteer Centre's certificate of appreciation. Family pictures are pasted onto the other pages—brothers and sisters, nieces and nephews he never sees.

"My family don't want nothing to do with me," Myles says quietly. It's because of his homosexuality and HIV. Still, Myles treasures their pictures. He wishes they'd bring their new babies around for him to look at. He closes the album sadly.

Myles's generosity isn't unusual. Ask any waitress who gives the best tips. Ask any store manager who spends more on their kids at Christmas. Ask the homeless guy on the corner who gives him more spare change. The poor make up close to a quarter of Canada's volunteers, subsidizing our social programs with their effort, their hours of hard work. It doesn't surprise me at all that Myles would volunteer in a community that shuns him. It's his deliberate act of optimism.

But optimism can't sustain him and Syd during the last days of the month before the welfare cheque. There's little to eat in the house: bread, frozen chips, two oranges, evaporated milk and Tang. If it weren't for the soup kitchen, Myles and Syd would literally starve. They get a free lunch at least three times a week, as do thousands of others across the nation: between 1500 and 1800 emergency food programs feed poor Canadians.

We walk with our collars pulled over our chins the few blocks to Ramiro House. It's a remarkably tidy, pleasant place. The staff dole out generous portions and they're friendly, like waiters, which is something to be truly grateful for. The people who eat here are bent close to their bowls, eyes on their food. They sit according to their afflictions: the rubbies, the jobless young men, the single moms, the psychiatric patients. The human need for tribal lines exists even here.

Myles and Syd take a table alone. The lunch is hearty: grilled cheese, soup, broccoli and carrots, turkey stew. Lillian, a short-haired blonde, comes close to the table and flirts with Syd. Today she's in a blue-and-yellow-braided commissionaire's uniform. Syd tries to disappear inside his coat. "I get scared that I'm going to end up here, that I'm going to be one of these people," he says, looking at Lillian.

Myles isn't as afraid of poverty. He lived most of his childhood on welfare. "My mom used to make what she called welfare stew," he laughs. "Baloney and vegetables all cooked up. It was great."

Myles worries about being alone—the absence of his family, the precarious love between him and Syd. He wants to get married. "There's this woman Donna we know. She's married other gays. She said she'd do it." Myles leans over the table and excitedly whispers his wedding plans to me: cold cuts and fancy little sandwiches and the grooms in basic black. Maybe a honeymoon camping. He grins like a kid. Syd's expression is much less definite.

Seven months later, Myles's welfare payment is reduced by $70 because of budget cuts. He weeps into the phone as he tells me.

TEN-CENT TOURS

Mmmm. I smell the late lilacs as a cool dew settles along the banks of the Saint John River. West of Fredericton she flows sweet and lazy and almost southern in her delicateness. Dusk is coming—terra-cotta light—and the land looks tender and good. I think of my mom's boy friend. He had a name for such pleasures: the ten-cent tour.

"Anyone want to go on a ten-cent tour?" Robbie would bellow throughout my childhood, waving us into the old white

Pontiac. It was a Sunday escape from our four small rooms: a country drive to confound his navigational skill and to impress our imaginations with the hugeness of the world. "Are we lost yet?" we'd ask and my mother would scowl and somehow Robbie would rescue the mood with a lovely view or the discovery of a hidden stand of pine. When there was money there were hot dogs, ice cream, maybe even cream soda from a roadside wagon. These afternoons were unhurried, unworried, fixed in my heart with the smell of hay and lilacs, the falling of shadows against our faces, the sound of wind and water. On the way home my mother would sing with her lilting voice and all arguments would be silenced. The adults would share something sweet up there in the front seat: a giggle, an uncomplicated moment of love. We'd come home tired and content from our ten-cent tour, certain of our love for each other.

MEDUCTIC: PARADISE LOST

In 1981 my friends Patty and Doug swore off the big city grind. They left Calgary, packed their van and drove across Canada, looking for paradise. Patty was seven-and-a-half months pregnant and by New Brunswick they were running out of highway. They stopped and put an ad in the local paper: "Family looking for work."

The job they got was on a sheep farm—a place to live but not much of a salary. Dougie heard about a retraining course, enrolled and became a certified shepherd. The farmer increased his wages and they've been living by their wits and inventiveness ever since.

When I pull into their place it's with the relief and anticipation of someone coming home. "How the hell are ya?" Patty

Doug *(left)* and Patty

hollers, waving a pair of scissors. She's cutting a neighbour's hair, part of the barter system out here; in exchange the woman lets her use her washer and dryer.

"You hungry? How long you staying? Holy shit, this is great, man. Want some of Dougie's brew?" At forty-two, Patty is athletic, exuberant, gabby as a girl.

The house is exactly how I imagined it—well built up, piece by piece. They bought it cheap, $16,000 with eight acres. There's lots of light and pine and a stunning view of the Saint John River.

I have to smile at their cupboardful of CBC mugs. "We got their T-shirts too. Dougie wins all the music questions on the radio call-ins. We run low and Dougie calls into a few contests."

Patty and Dougie enjoy life pared down and snail paced. "What's the rush?" Dougie asks, passing me a joint as we sink into the low-slung Victorian couch. "I figured a while back that there's really nowhere to get to. You're already there."

Dougie's a pensive, bearded man, a watcher of people who's

amused by contradiction and hurry. We chuckle over the poisonous ambitions of our own generation, the insatiable hungers. Patty and Doug's appetites are naturally meagre: a decent sound system, a few pairs of jeans, some Eric Clapton, a car that works, a back shed to putter in. And lots of time for the kids. The children sparkle with the attention. Melissa and Chris are emotionally secure, responsible, curious, undulled by excess and television.

But geography intrudes on the best plans. The only work in the area is half time, part time or short term, which would suit them fine if there were more of it. Dougie's been selling exhaust systems for the last two months, travelling the Maritimes a few days a week. He doesn't like the work, but it's necessary. He's being employed under a training program—his boss and the government share the cost of his salary forty-sixty.

"Don't know what I'm being trained for really," Dougie says ironically. "I know how to sell and I know how to drive. What I don't know is what job's waitin' for me after this one."

Life's becoming another kind of treadmill—government training programs and UI. Patty and Dougie haven't squandered a single opportunity to get rehauled, retrained and retreaded. Patty's earned three certificates from the government: she's a qualified nursing assistant, hairdresser and barber.

"You got to try to make things work for yourself," Patty insists. "Some people around here are just wasting away. Like, 'Hey death, hurry up.' " But there's a futility even to Patty's resolve. There's no real job at the end of her effort. She's got her name in with the local ambulance company and the in-home nursing people for fill-in work. Her regular job is part-time waitressing, which you don't need a government certificate for.

"We got employers now can't or won't hire unless you're on

a government program," Dougie explains. "Way cheaper for them. My boss got me on this thirty-four-week thing 'cause he can't afford to pay me $400 a week, which is what leaving my family for three days and nights is worth."

In five months Dougie's boss will tell him he doesn't have the money to pay his full salary. Dougie will have to choose between taking a pay cut or looking for other work. "What's the point training for a job that doesn't exist? Or for a dead-end job with a built-in pink slip?" Dougie wonders. It's a struggle against futility that he shares with many Canadians.

Over 420,000 unemployed workers were funnelled from UI to job-training schemes in 1991-92. After classroom study, apprenticeships and temporary job placements, almost half the participants didn't find employment. Some programs are in fact a subsidy for business, a kind of corporate welfare. Employers get their pick of workers for free or at salaries that are split with the government. Many of them don't bother to offer any training; they just want someone to do their grunt work or sweep their floors. And as for hiring later, why should they? When the program's finished they just order another worker through another program. And people like Doug and Patty never earn the right to permanent, decently waged work.

"We're thinking of moving to Charlottetown," Patty tells me. "We figure there's five years' worth of work coming if the fixed link goes through. We're thinking a restaurant might be good, something for the tourists and the workers."

"I'm gonna check either side of the fixed link," Dougie says. "Look at the possibilities."

Eleven years after escaping city life, Patty and Dougie are being driven back. They may have survived rural isolation, boredom, even the wagging of small-town tongues, but what

they can't live without is real work. What's paradise without a
sense of meaning and usefulness?

CAMPBELLTON: IT'S A WONDERFUL LIFE

Babe *(left)* and Scouter

The chubby kid with the Dough-Boy face and squinting eyes is
waving at traffic, shaking a glassful of something. All the kids
are. For a small stretch of road Campbellton feels like a Third
World country with its pesky curbside hucksters. Some are just
earning candy money but there are a few earning a living. I pull
in alongside the boy and see his father sitting in the ditch on an
overturned shopping cart. The boy rushes up, with unevenly
cut hair, a torn shirt and a fat, open face. He's selling hazelnuts,
$2.50 a glassful.

"Me and me boys picks 'em," the father says. "Takes a

coupla days in the bush other side of Sugar Loaf. That there's Babe and this's my other boy . . ." He digs in his pocket and pulls out a walletful of pictures.

The man's a dark-eyed Acadian with the slow deliberate-ness of a western movie star. He's got big working-man hands and baggy black pants stuffed into gum boots. He looks like an overgrown Huck Finn.

Babe keeps sliding into the ditch towards us, wanting to be part of the conversation, but his father gently shoos him back. "Sell yer nuts dere, Babe, thatta boy."

It's been a year since the man was laid off from the ceme-tery. He'd been four years digging graves; now he's run out of UI. "In the summer I take odd jobs, mowing lawns, taking tourists up the mountain. "

"Winter ya do snow removal, Dad," Babe cuts in.

"Dat's right, Babe." And then remembering, "Get back up there, Babe, show em yer nuts."

"Babe there's what you call almost born outa wedlock." The boy grins, enjoying the attention. The man met his wife when she was a secretary at the vet's.

"I brought me dog in and that was it. We started goin' around. Then we got Babe comin'."

"And then you got married, right, Dad?"

"That's right, Babe. Keep shakin' dose nuts."

"We've had our ups and downs." It's obvious there's a coldness that's grown between husband and wife. The man won't say anything more about her, preferring to keep his dis-appointment to himself.

"Sometimes it gets boring here. I got my name in eighteen places, haven't heard from a one since. But I climb up to the top of Sugar Loaf, sometimes even bring my sun chair, and there's when I breathe and relax and watch them teeny tiny cars passing. That's where I get my name, Scouter. 'Cause I'm a scouter.

"Would ya like me and Babe could show you Sugar Loaf tomorrow?"

The next day I'm a little late. I find Scouter's old single-gear bicycle by the side of the highway, and a few seconds later Scouter appears. He's been picking hazelnuts—already filled up half the bag slung across his shoulder.

"I'm sorry. I'd have called but I didn't have your number."

"Don't have a phone. The wife doesn't like 'em."

Scouter's alone; there's no sign of Babe.

"He woke up sick, sore throat."

Suddenly Scouter is strange to me and I become afraid. We're too alone, he's too alone, intense. Impulsively I invent a cockeyed story about having to meet a couple of BIG MEN at the foot of the mountain in an hour, hoping to ward off evil intentions. Scouter says nothing. We begin our climb, walking along the gravel jogging path that circles the base of Sugar Loaf.

"Me, I knows this better than my own hand and if I were to ever leave I'd have to find myself another best friend. Been comin' here since I was twelve." Scouter walks taller here, with a proprietary ease.

"Dere's where I met my first girl friend," he says, pointing through the treetops, "at the top. Thought I looked sad and I was going to jump. We both laughed at the time."

Scouter knows every secret of this mountain—what grows here, what won't, the shortcuts and invisible paths. He's roamed its back side and front side. At the top is where he builds his fires in the winter. "Me, I even bring tea sometimes. Winter's a fine time here, especially Christmas. I like to see the tiny lights twinkling on the houses."

The mountain watches Scouter, warns him like a friend.

"Sugar Loaf even saved me from drinkin'. Never smoked but started into drinking too much. One day I went to the liquor store right down there, I looked up at her, turned around and bought two big bottles of Coke instead. I came up with my boy Babe. Never drank since."

Suddenly, rabbit quick, Scouter steps off the path into the trees. It's a steep shortcut through the woods on a sunken path. Our talking's spare, lean, Scouter staying silent like a hired man. He stops and yanks at a sapling, snapping its ends off, then handing it to me for a walking stick. I falter often, but he never touches me, only stops to give encouragement and to let me catch my breath.

"Just a few more minutes to the steps, then clear sailin' after dat."

The mountainside is barer higher up, but no easier to climb. Scouter moves steadily, unhurriedly, watching things I cannot see. He stops abruptly at one of his favourite ledges and we rest.

"I want to work, you know," he says suddenly. He must have been mulling this over all the way up. "I got ads in the paper to do handy work, lawn mowing, snow removal. I use my friend's plough. But I got no phone, somebody ran up a big bill. So they got to call my friend or come looking for me. Some of the hotels know me, send visitors to me for a trip up the mountain.

"I done all kinds of work. Graveyard, construction, horse stable, I was even a part-time wrestler. Did it nights for the money but I jumped from some scaffolding and hurt four discs."

It was Sugar Loaf that helped Scouter shake off the extra bulk after he quit wrestling. He was 295 pounds. When his back cleared up, he ran up and down the mountain and sweated off 100 pounds.

We start the last ascent, hauling ourselves up the steepest part, when Scouter spots blueberries. "Nature's candy I call dat. 'Tink I'll come tomorrow and pick some of dose." It's as good as finding loose change to Scouter, something more to sell on the side of the road.

He's hurrying me along now, eager to get to the top. We crawl finally on to the scraggy summit of metal cables and transmission towers. It isn't Eden at all—it's desolate, lunar, with scattered eruptions of rock and technology. I'm vaguely disappointed.

We stumble to the edge to catch our breath and fill our lungs with wind. Campbellton seems so tiny, benign, so sweetly untroubled and harmless. This is what Scouter comes for: the deceptive feeling of weightlessness at the top of a mountain. There's a sense of possibility, of resurrection. And an urge to confess.

"Sometimes I come up here just to lose myself." Scouter speaks absently, in a low, slow voice. "It's crossed my mind to end it up here, to just jump. I tries to get myself clear, but something always comes along, something I got no money for. When my boy got sick I came up here and I stood there looking down, thinking how I could just jump. But I couldn't leave my boys, couldn't leave 'em alone in the world. When I came down there was a man at the bottom. I told him about my boy and he said he had some work he could give me, make something for a day's labour. And I got the money and things went okay."

We both stare silently into the horizon. It is something when a man like Scouter reveals his heart. He doesn't want to be touched or held. He wants to be listened to by a stranger who brings no history or expectation. Maybe we sit two minutes, maybe five or ten. The silence is comfortable, safe.

"I come up to the top to sit and write my diary. Sometimes I even talk to myself, asking myself questions, giving myself answers . . . You know what?"

"What?"

"Nobody ran up a bill on my phone. I owe $400 and it's been cut off."

"That's okay. There aren't any big guys waiting for me at the bottom."

A small smile passes between us.

"Me, I don't wanna be poor, I don't wanna be rich, I just wanna be in the middle. I seen what money does to people and I seen what not having money does to people. I just wanna be in the middle so's I don't stick out and people won't look at me or my clothes. And so's I got enough fer my kids."

Slowly, steadily, Scouter and I walk together down his healing mountain. Back home to his boys.

CARING MUSIC

I'm enjoying a late breakfast at the downtown Woolworth in Campbellton: $2.25 and everything's good except for the Styrofoam plate. Stout, motherly Muriel the waitress tries to wedge me into the counter-side conversation. The old farmer beside me is clucking about the cost of things and cursing the unemployment.

"Only CN and the hospitals are hiring. And a bit of salmon fishing. Not like before." Muriel lifts her chin and stares sadly at a young amputee at the cash across the aisle. "Hard to see that on a young boy. And we complain!"

She spins on her heel and turns up the radio, as if that might block out the world's agonies. It's a country station, amateurish—the woman DJ keeps forgetting to turn off her mike. Now she's announcing the wrong song. Then a man talks with a smoky voice, in a language I've never heard before.

"It's the Micmac station," Muriel tells me. "Best in the area. None of that stupid talk. And lots of country."

Where's it from?

"Comes from up there on the reserve." On the Quebec side of Chaleur Bay.

"Real caring music. I like it."

CENTRAL

I enter now the complex city-states bulging with new arrivals, the one-industry towns falling to their knees. So many claims are tentative here, so many people come with their dreams to do the grunt work. The factory jobs are gone or going. Many working people are a pay cheque away from poverty. City sidewalks belong to the people who live on them. There is a decay in the centre of the country, a collapsing of infrastructures. Cities and towns stagger into debt, disparities between rich and poor are gaping. Poverty is overt and desperate.

QUEBEC: MON PAYS C'EST L'HIVER

I'd forgotten how beautiful Quebec is—the northern silence, the water and woods, the soft southern river banks full of bones and stories.

But the province is so seldom geography to me, so much more a state of mind and mood. French is my mother's tongue, my mother tongue, the language of my hands and heart. I've lived here, left here, and always return divided in myself, thin-skinned, contrary, defending my other selves. Quebec is home, a place to rebel against, a place not quite forgiven. But she is lovely. And shockingly poorer than when I left her five years ago.

Almost half a million Quebecers are unemployed at the end of 1992. The manufacturing sector has been virtually obliterated. Every day, 60,000 Montrealers depend on food handouts. The province has responded with some of the most regressive welfare legislation in Canada, forcing recipients into work-fare programs disguised as training. These are illegal under the Canada Assistance Plan, violating federal welfare standards. But who dares criticize Quebec at this time in our history? And who else suffers but the poor? The province is using the poor, their cheap labour, to entice investment and fuel an economic recovery.

As I travel across one of my favourite places, I see not so much a war on poverty as a war on poor people. Traditionally Quebecers have manoeuvred around their social obstacles with deftness, humour and political skill. But there's an ideological narrowing in government, a retaliatory sensibility. The poor are being frightened into silence, growing exhausted, cynical, forgetful. Public faith is eroding as poverty spreads and government punishes. If citizens become afraid to participate, to dissent, the state ignores them and leaders dictate. I can feel those cold winds in Quebec. It's the beginning of a winter of silence.

RESTIGOUCHE: VOICE OF THE MICMAC

Some of the deepest, ugliest, most chronic poverty in Canada is on native reserves. One third of reserve homes have no running water. More than half have no central heating. The squalor and deprivation are Third World, the legacy of hate and exclusion.

Johnny Bone

In fact, our Indian Act was the model for the South African laws that forced blacks into separate homelands.

Reserves hold people hostage, retard development, impose dependency, institutionalize poverty. Indians may own their land or homes, but chartered banks don't accept reserve property as collateral for loans. Natives are shut out of the white economy. Welfare dependency on reserves can run as high as 95 per cent. Native people have a life expectancy rate that's eight years less than whites, and their babies die twice as often.

These are the convulsing remains of a dismembered, discarded society. Centuries of exclusion and suppression of native values have left social scars and empty spaces. That First Nations Canadians aren't crushed completely is a tribute to their cultural resilience. There's a native instinct towards balance and reconciliation, a vitality that's ignored and diminished. I see it in the faces of the Annishnawbe—"the people." I also see suspicion.

I follow the trail of a Micmac man's voice. The highway into Quebec crumbles at the edge of the Restigouche Reserve. Dusty, unpaved roads lead me into the ruins of old history. Micmac have lived on the Gaspé Peninsula for 2500 years. Yet their biggest monument is foreign—the Catholic church of Ste-Anne de Restigouche, the patron saint of the Bretons who washed up on these shores in the middle of the eighteenth century. The names in the graveyard speak of conversions and cultural eclipse: Metallic, Condo, Moses Canoe.

I drive slowly around the potholes, noticing the watchfulness, the slight hostility, the poverty. Restigouche looks better off than many reserves: tidy, evenly painted. But most of the residents are unemployed, and more than half are on welfare. Children smile easily, unafraid of my strangeness. But older eyes watch, wondering what my business is.

I find the radio station—CHRQ-FM—in a skinny clapboard house on the main highway. The sign on the door reads: "Play It Loud, Play It Proud." Upstairs, the man with the smoky voice sits in a tiny sound booth cranking out country music. Sixty-year-old Johnny Bone is an old-fashioned man with gentle manners, bent over the control board. He's uncomfortably tall for this little room. "This station means everything to me. It's our station, Indian people, the reserve people. I believe in that."

Johnny Bone built most of the radio station by himself last year. For free. The management had been looking for volunteer builders. He was the only one to show up. "I wasn't working. I just came in and tole 'em I was a carpenter," he shrugs, smiling his slightly rakish grin.

He juts out his chin and surveys the rooms with immense pride. "I didn't tell 'em I'd never built before. They didn't ask. I just prayed to God 'cause I'm a Catholic, and I got through it."

Johnny Bone has worked many jobs: the army, construction, ironworks, even his own delivery business. He's still out of work so he volunteers seven days a week on his Micmac show. "It's mostly for the old people. That's their language. The young ones want to learn now and that's good, but it's the language of here. It's not much good outside. When I was a boy it's all I knew, what we spoke at home. But it held me back 'cause when I went to school I had to learn English."

Johnny Bone's the keeper of the cultural flame, the guide to the old ways, the one who remembers. It's that memory the young ones reach for, or invent if they have to, to affirm their place in the world. "I don't go for the new ways of these kids. They're bringin' sweet grass and all that. It's good for them, gives 'em pride, I guess. But that's not the way I was brought up. I don't want any of that Warrior Society stuff."

Johnny Bone believes that rage only binds people temporarily. Culture, self-esteem, personal effort hold them permanently. He learned this from his mother, in a generation before Native assertiveness and political clout. His voice softens talking about her. She had a hard life—thirteen when she married, ten kids, dirt poor. During the war years she cleaned the houses of the rich over in Campbellton for ration cards. "Just for the damned stamps," Johnny Bone says with rare bitterness.

"But my mother was an incredible woman. She believed in puttin' something back into the community. No matter how tired she was." During the war years she sold window decals for the Red Cross, $1 each, for the war effort. She went on foot, door to door, over miles of countryside.

Johnny Bone can see her as he stares at a piece of wall, and his eyes fill with tears. Those were years of love and hurt and deep, deep shame. He hated their poverty, wanting, like a good son, to give his mother a better world. I wonder if he fears being poor again, if his long unemployment is cutting into him, opening old wounds.

"I'm not poor," he says emphatically. "I get whatchya might call an honorarium from the radio station because they want to give it to me." It is not charity.

Johnny Bone's living on his savings, though there's not as much as there used to be. "My kids don't want for anything. And my land's mine. I'm not poor."

On the way out of the station I read a poster with the words of Chief Dan George: "Let no one forget it . . . we are a people with special rights guaranteed to us by promises and treaties. We do not beg for these rights, nor do we thank you . . . . We do not thank you for them because we paid for them . . . and God help us the price we paid was exorbitant! We paid for them with our culture, our dignity and self-respect. We paid and paid and paid until we became a beaten race, poverty-stricken and conquered."

MIGUASHA: THE EXPENDABLES

I drive slowly past the rolling red land that Johnny Bone's mother tramped through, peddling her war crosses. The countryside falls into Baie des Chaleurs, fertile and stunning. I think about Johnny Bone's pride, his refusal to be labelled. It's difficult to count the poor when they themselves are reluctant to be counted. But who wants to be counted poor? To be poor still means to be failed, defective, marginal. People always insist that there are poorer citizens, meaner circumstances, harder times elsewhere. It's sometimes a deflective gesture that allows them their pride. It's also a measure of gratitude for the true riches of their lives: family, community, a sense of usefulness. These are the things that count.

I am many miles from Johnny Bone when I stop for food at Parc Miguasha. There's something peculiar here, strange angles to the moods, the faces of the customers. They're all women, some vacant-eyed, some twitching with a private busyness, others staring with alarming intensity. A prim old lady sits by the window in her sun bonnet, insisting on a self locked back in the 1940s. There's a Bohemian-looking woman, sixtyish, with a gash of red lipstick and severe black bangs, chain-smoking. Two others fuss ecstatically over dessert at the lunch counter, luxuriating in the extravagance of spending. *"En ville, c'est un dollar dix*—in town it's a dollar ten," someone complains about the juice. "Mais ici, it's one tirty."

Finally I realize they're psychiatric patients. From Campbellton, out on a day trip. For all their faulty wiring, they're managing to keep up an incessant chatter in both French and English. It's a wonderful word-weave, demonstrating a proficiency most of our high-paid politicians lack.

In the centre of the noise, at the middle table, joking and encouraging, sit the three custodians. Joel and Michel are Acadians, middle-aged men in casual knit sweaters. Ann, about forty, is in a girlish skirt and blouse. I peg her as Irish.

"Yeah. Howdja know?" The eyes. Blazing, hungry, cautious. Anne has pain and experience scratched into her face, a pinched and haunted look from long times without. And a huge smile that softens all the hurt. She was probably born poor.

"How's the work?" I venture.

"Part-time."

"You like it that way?"

"No," she giggles defensively. "No." Her wages, like those of two million other part-time workers, aren't enough to live on.

The Bohemian Woman moves to the table, insisting on being included. Ann hands her a cigarette as small, balding Joel takes a turn explaining: "Dere's nutting we can do. De hospital don't want to give de part-time people contracts. We gut no syndicate, no benefits and no security."

"And we don't get overtime," Ann reminds him.

"Dat's it. Sometimes we work eighty hours in a week and dere's no overtime."

Ann jumps in. "See, if they don't give us a contract we can't get into the union. So there's less pay and less protections. And the way they do it is they hire us five months atta time."

"And lots of times dey don't even call us in de five monts," Michel adds.

"And ya know what the saddest part is?" Ann asks. "Maybe we could go somewheres else, but these people can't. All these staff and budget cutbacks and the patients aren't even getting their cigarette money any more. It's us that's givin' 'em smokes outa our own packs." On cue, the Bohemian Woman sticks out her hand.

"*Si vous plaît?*"

"It stinks, but what can ya do?" Ann shrugs. "I've had worse jobs." She had to go to Ontario to find work a few years back. One of the jobs was cleaning crud from a factory floor. She peels back her shirt and reveals the blistering skin of her mid-chest. It looks like a burn wound. "It cracks like that whenever I get direct sunlight. Happened after I worked at the plant."

I can't stop staring at the sore. Ann quickly buttons her collar, embarrassed by my shock.

"They told me to clean up the goo on the factory floor. Said

I only had to work an hour a day and that I'd get paid fer a full day's work. Sounded great."

I feel myself being yanked through the cracks of my own safe thinking, my own insistent faith, sucked into another century, into some parallel world of starker patterns. It's an unfamiliar Canada. Ann has been marked by birth or circumstances as one of the disposable ones. It's just that simple. And that obscene.

"If you'd known it might cause this rash, maybe even something worse, would you still have done it?"

She smiles sheepishly. "I needed the money." After a long silence she adds, "Probably not."

I'll meet many more of the disposable poor on my travels, but it's Ann's wounds that will haunt me most. That horrible, bubbling raw sore just above her breasts.

ST-SIMÉON: APPALACHIA

Left to right: Marielle, Kevin, Karin and Eve

I cross the Saint-Laurent by ferry and arrive into the rattling chaos of St-Siméon. It's a small harbour town, straight from the heart and full of hope: cluttered, utilitarian, a jumble of touristy conveniences. The ferry deposits her human cargo and locals appear on the highway with bags full of blueberries. The tourists stop for directions, snacks, then hurry along their way, leaving a few dollars behind. St-Siméon returns to her silence and the vendors vanish from the road.

This is the federal riding of Charlevoix, former prime minister Brian Mulroney's constituency. It's mostly bush and water, and there's not much work.

As I drive north along Route 138 I'm startled by a familiar row of flimsy houses and ragged children squatting in the dirt. It's a smudgy, Appalachian poverty from a half century ago— not one I've lived, but still familiar. I know this place instinctively, intimately—it belongs to my mother, to her childhood, images I've carried in my heart for years. I stare at the past, a little dumbfounded on this seam between generations, between memories.

The children watch open-mouthed as I drive up, and a thin woman pokes her head out of the front door, delighted at the prospect of company.

"*Bonjour, bonjour*," she says heartily. Marielle is only twenty-three. She tells me right away.

"*Et, tu penses que je suis trop jeune pour avoir beaucoup d'enfants?*"—you must think I'm young to have so many children?

Yep.

Marielle's three kids are extraordinarily filthy and dressed in old clothes. Little Kevin smells of urine. There aren't any books or toys, so the children play with grown-up things: their father's tools and engine parts. But they're curious, happy, loved. Marielle is unselfconscious in a stained nighty, crocheted slippers and uncombed hair. There's a playful shrug to her, a Trudeauesque, hands-in-the-air resignation that's wise, tired and amused. She sits in her rocking chair on the porch, enjoying my sudden arrival.

Marielle has lived on the side of the highway all her life. Her parents are next door, an aunt is on the other side of them. Cousins, offspring, siblings all cram into each other's lives, sharing the monthly mortgage on the land. Her home is a rickety trailer with a precious front porch. Inside is dark and untidy and small. Outside there's dirt—no lawn, no landscaping, just a few wild blueberries.

Marielle's husband grew up across the highway, "*Là*"—there, she points, laughing at my amusement. They married when she was only seventeen. "*C'est normal ici*. Big families and young brides." Marielle's father came from a brood of twenty-six kids, her mother from one of ten.

"*J'adore ça*," she says breezily. "I was only one time to Quebec City. Nowhere else big. I didn't like it. In the big winter storms, when there aren't any cars on the highway, the silence is wonderful. That's when I feel myself." She rolls the words in her mouth luxuriously, almost tasting the time of it.

Marielle and her husband are just about the only ones in their circle of friends not on welfare.

"My husband worked three years in an ironworks plant, making furniture in Quebec City. Then he got laid off. Now he works at the hunting reserve, cutting trees in the summer."

In the winters there's *chômage*—UI. But spring and summer have been bad this year. Lots of young people have left looking for work. The ones who stay compete with her husband for jobs. "And so wet," Marielle grimaces. "There weren't even any forest fires to give the men work. Usually there's thirty or forty of them by now."

She peppers me with questions.

"Are there French people in Toronto?"

"Is there work?"

"What kind?"

"How much do they pay?"

"How expensive is it to live there?"

These are exact questions demanding exact answers. Marielle is inching towards the bigger world, looking for a route out of poverty. She and her husband are even considering welfare for the first time. One of the boys has asthma. He needs a special pump and refills every fifteen days. It costs $21 a shot. Welfare gives recipients drug cards. They could save a lot of cash. But for Marielle there's the problem of privacy, of having welfare people snooping into her life. And all the rules.

"*C'est pas la liberté*"—it's just not freedom. Even if there are ways around it. Marielle's parents have been on welfare ever since her father hurt his back a few years ago. Welfare doesn't allow recipients to own cars worth over $5000, so her mother gets the car salesman to fake the receipt. "And you're not supposed to own expensive things like vcrs. So everybody hides them."

Marielle's casualness is almost comical. She's completely blind to the fact that many people would call this cheating. But whose money is it anyway? Welfare recipients aren't wards of the state just because the state supports them. They're not supposed to forfeit their right to choice because they're financially dependent. If they want to spend their money on luxury items, why not? Everyone else does. If someone wants a colour tv and is willing to starve for a month to get it, that's her business. The state can't legislate against stupidity. And unlike big business, the poor can't keep going back to the public trough when they've spent all their money. There's no mechanism for that in the welfare system. If their children suffer or go hungry, then we have a responsibility to step in. But that's not about poverty, that's child protection. Somehow, though, we've held on to our Victorian attitudes about the poor's right to enjoyment, indulgence, material comforts. Poverty's supposed to be about suffering. People who don't hurt badly enough, who manage a certain level of comfort, are undeserving.

"*Aye*, away *là, va t'en*"—go on, git! Marielle hollers at the kids, then collapses laughing. Her children are in my car, pilfering my chocolate bars, yanking out my film rolls, tape recorder, Swiss Army knife, Kotex pads. That's what gets Marielle and me screeching. But the children are oblivious. Marielle feigns anger, cleans the gobs of chocolate off my car and locks the car doors. With a satisfied grin she leans against the hood and holds her hand out to one of the boys.

"*Donne ça à maman*"—give that to Mommy. But little Yves doesn't want to part with his chocolate. "*Yves, donne ça à maman.*" Yves hang-doggedly gives up his chocolate and shuffles away. "*Merci, mon chou*"—thanks, sweetie. Marielle pops the candy in her mouth, throwing the wrapper on the ground. She sighs loudly.

"*Ben, j'sais pas*"—I don't know, she says with a shrug. "The rich have less heart than the poor. They miss a lot." She looks around smugly at her grimy, kid-infested yard. What she sees is very different from what I see. It pleases her. And fills her up with pride.

STE-ANNE-DE-BEAUPRÉ: LE PRINCE DE PHILOSOPHIE

Normand stands like a broken saint at the edge of Ste-Anne-de-Beaupré, waving a limp wrist at the passing traffic. I circle back,

Normand

not sure if he's hitchhiking or possessed by a vision. After all, this is the Lourdes of Quebec, a communion of religious excess and low-down hucksterism. I was trying to avoid it. Now I'm stuck behind a convoy of yellow school buses filled with tourists. The old, the infirm, the wild-eyed gape at the shop windows full of Madonnas and Jesus pennants, anxious to spend at the carnival of piety.

Normand is even more beguiling close up, all elbows and angles: a Don Quixote in his battered straw hat and crumpled white linen suit with dead flowers hanging out of the pocket. And the gentlest blue eyes and smile.

"*Je suis un voyageur*," he whispers. But only in the summer. He scurries back to Amqui, his home in the Gaspésie, for winter welfare. He used to be a draughtsman; he quit that fifteen years ago to take up travelling and poetry.

"*Ah, un roi de philosophie*"—a philosopher king, I tease.

"*Non. Seulement le fils*," he chuckles. I'm only the king's son.

"I live up there, in the bush," he tells me, sweeping his hand with an exhausted majesty over the hills beside us. There are berries, fruits and the quiet he craves for his poetry.

He's a calm, warm, lovely man, and I ease into his tranquillity. Perhaps he's forty, perhaps sixty. It's the face of madness or divinity. Maybe both. "Are you a religious man?" I ask.

"*Oui, je suis religieux,*" he says, doubting what I mean by my question. He's obviously not a frothing evangelical. "I've returned to the powers of Mary and Jesus. I lost my belief because of bad storytellers. But it's been cleared and I've returned to a true belief.

"I hate these philosophers and writers," he says, suddenly enraged. "I stamp on their papers and crush it into the ground to be swallowed by forgetfulness." He must have believed in them strongly at one time to be provoked into such anger.

He pulls a round of soft cheese from his pocket and offers me some. "You know what's killing us? Cars. They are driving over our lives. Pulling out our intestines. We must feed them roads and shopping malls. We are all serving them, becoming dead."

"But you hitchhike," I argue. "You travel in other people's cars."

"It is one of the smaller contradictions I must live with." Normand smiles impishly and for a brief second I'm tempted to trade places with him.

MONTREAL: ISLAND OF MEMORIES

Montreal holds many of my myths and memories. I can't help smiling as I cross the Jacques Cartier Bridge, as much for the preciousness of my time here as for my ability to escape. I was poor, sometimes hungry, in this city, making art and love at the beginning of my adult self. I drive, remembering food and lovers more than anything else: the cheap Vietnamese places on Prince Arthur, the souvlaki on St-Viateur, the scrumptious chicken at La Cabane on St-Laurent. It was a good city to be poor in then, tolerant, humorous, embracing, imposing little shame.

We were apprenticing artists, activists, slackers—honing our craft and our excuses, inventing ourselves. Some of us were born poor, others middle class. We all assumed meagre appetites and renounced conventional comforts. We lived in run-down flats and garrets in Little Burgundy, Plateau Mont Royal, Mile End, feeding ourselves on the free food from gallery shows and book launches. We sprayed graffiti on the sides of banks—"*Mange les riches*"—eat the rich!

Poverty was a defining part of our culture, a mark of membership, a badge of pride. There were shadows on our optimism, occasional humiliations that tore through our posturing. I remember the hydro bastards with their boots in my door, preventing me from shutting it. They had no right to enter my apartment, to stop my service in the winter, but the five of them marched into my home, shut off the power and grinned at my embarrassment.

But mostly Montreal was forgiving of us. And we could live well and dream well in the city she used to be.

LITTLE BURGUNDY: GOOD NEIGHBOURS

Remember the Wise Ones who ruled our poor neighbourhoods with cranky common sense and kindness? The curb sweepers and keepers of the peace, the gossip queens, who demanded the best of us? Some were nosy parkers—shrill and chattering. Others

Miss May

lived in the shadows, quiet, watchful, speaking in small gestures and raised eyebrows. Too many have gone, pushed into
oblivion by the wrecker's ball and the new tyranny of individu-
alism. They've been replaced by Neighbourhood Watch, Block
Parents, Crime Stoppers. At one time, though, it was these wise
women, peeping through their curtains, who guarded our
streets and kept them safe. And Christ be weeping if you
crossed them or told a lie, because they could see right into your
soul.

I knew such a Wise One: a slight, silent, tightly wound spool
of a woman who kept a rooming house in Overdale. Miss May
ran the place for a penny-pinching cheat. Thirty-two years she
tended the flotsam, the old, the dying, loving them when everyone else forgot to. She scrubbed the place almost bare of its
paint, and managed the house and neighbourhood with tolerance and forgiveness. Miss May believed in second chances but
never third ones.

I look for her now but there's only a hole where the house

used to stand. I knock at a door and an old neighbour knows where she's gone. "Miss May? Over the tracks in Little Burgundy." In the new rent-controlled apartments.

The drive is grim. What used to be an industrial part of the city is now a bald patch of concrete and square brown boxes. When will these urban renewal people figure out what a real neighbourhood looks like? Not even the trees—scrawny, shadeless, newly planted—give comfort or colour. All the character of the old community has been erased—there's no corner store or greasy spoon, no stoop or step or bench to pause and share a story on. The borders have disappeared too; the poor people from Overdale are crammed in with all kinds of other rejects: the old, infirm, deranged. It's a place of strangers, instant and institutionalized. The city calls it rejuvenation.

"We had our ways of keepin' out de troublemakers and unmixables. Now we got de government doin' a bad job of it." Miss May looks worn down. She's gotten skinnier and frailer—hunched over. But her attitude's still no guff, spit-in-yer-eye. And her bullshit barometer's working fine. "We got druggies and crazies coming trough de walls, living wit us gang from Overdale. We're stayin' in mostly. Scared."

Miss May sits in her chair by the window, a ghostly silhouette in a changing world. These streets don't belong to her any more. They don't bring the chatter and clatter of neighbours coming by for tea or a couple of borrowed bucks. Miss May moved here with her Christian kindness. But the street pushed her back inside.

"I kept up my Meals on Wheels. No car, just went on foot carrying a basketa meals for de old people. Went into one place nearby here, come out and dere were a coupla fellas figured I had money in my basket. One grabs me by de arm. I says, 'Mind yer own business.' I'm kickin' him and he puts me against de wall and punches me hard, twice in de chest. Took de wind right outa me, but I managed to crawl outa de hall and outside. Dat put an end to my walking de streets." At sixty-nine her bones are too brittle to be pushing off punks.

But Miss May insists on being useful. "I still answer de phones at Dave's place." Dave owns the lock and electrical shop on Guy Street. For free? "Yeah, fer free. A favour does a favour. He doesn't speak French so I do de phones and sometimes de counter. Known him thirty years from de area. And when it's my turn, he takes me around for my shoppin' or drives me here an' dere. Anyting I need."

But a lot of time is spent at home. Life is more remembered now than lived. Her apartment's covered with photographs: the faces of ex-roomers, neighbours and her favourite saint, Brother André. But there's dust over everything. Miss May's too tired to clean any more, and there isn't the same shame to a dirty house that there used to be. It's not like turning your back on God. Still, I coax her into letting me clean a little and she accepts reluctantly. With wet hands and rags and the familiar smell of ammonia in our noses, we begin our scrubbing and our house-work talk—the centuries-old babble of women, a stream of con-sciousness: feelings, memories, anecdotes that pass tribal wisdoms down through the generations. This is the old Miss May, and I'm happier than I've been in days.

"Did I tell ya 'bout the convent?" she chatters. "I was four-teen. Entered de Order of de Good Shepherds in 1938. All de poor families did dat. I stayed nine years. Got all my ribbons, became a Child of Mary. Den a novice."

It was a rigorous, lonely environment for a child. Credits were earned and lost for trivial matters—clinking cutlery could cancel the points required to move upward into heaven. Maybe it was at the convent she learned to walk so softly, noiselessly, afraid of causing God offence.

"I never went to school. I learned to read a little from my catechism, and also trough dem comic books. All we did was work. Up at four, mass at five, and den work till supper. We washed 2400 shirts a day, dat's how dey made dere money, doin' de rich people's laundry. We weren't allowed no talkin' till supper, den twenty minutes of it and to bed. I got my novice's ribbon on December 8, Immaculate Conception Day." She smiles remembering herself as a girl.

"Dey called me Sister Grace and shaved my head bald as a cue ball. Now why'd you tink God would want a girl shaved bald? Dey said it was our sacrifice."

Miss May suddenly stiffens and her voice turns hard. "I never went to school. I was always stupid. Best ting I knew was work, cleaning, janitor. I worked thirty-two years at de house; it was my home. In de end de city tore it down and none of us could save it. All dose years de boss never paid into a pension. And nuttin' I can do about it."

Miss May's poverty now follows her into old age, as it does almost half of single women over sixty-five. Miss May blinks hard and shakes her head in deep disappointment. She's been lied to and cheated most of her life, starting at the convent. When her mother died and she had to return home, the nuns sat her down.

"Dey told me terrible tings. Said *tous les hommes sont des cochons, cochons, garde-toi bien*"—all men are pigs; watch yourself. "And make your confession. Dey scared de shit outa me. Brainwashing, dat's what dey did—fill you full of fear. I was ascared fer years after dat. When I come out I knew nuttin' about nuttin' but work. Didn't even know what was in a man's pants. I called what I got on de top my angels and what I got on de bottom, I called Molly. Imagine!"

Miss May never did marry or have children. But she shook off her Catholic fright, broke through the dogma to a truly Christian tolerance and compassion. She took single mothers and homosexuals into the rooming house when everyone else refused them.

"I seen black wit white, white wit brown. I seen the overseas girls get in the family way and leave our place. I even gave one of 'em $1000 to send her back where she come from. And I had a few homosexuals in my place. Dora downstairs, she hates 'em, says all dem fuckin' homos should be wit women. Her own brudder Joe's a homosexual, always was welcomed here. We even had a homosexual club across de street in de old house, usta watch over our place. Good people."

A couple of years ago Miss May was asked to open her heart to a stranger: "De hospital where I usta volunteer called me up wit a special case. Said dere was a fella only I could help. He had de AIDS. Come from a big family and not a one of 'em at his side, too ashamed. Imagine? So I went to visitin' wit him, brought a Coke in case he wanted a sip, brought some smokes, tought he'd like a puff. Oh, I made him laugh on my stories of de old times, how poor we were. One day he tells me soft, 'Hold me, Mommy'—he called me Mommy. I held him and he slipped away in my arms like dat. His family finally come and I told his mother right to her face, 'You brought dat boy into de world, you shoulda been wit him when he left it.' She was ashamed. People kept away from dat boy. Even my own said I shoulda been scareda catchin' someting. All he wanted was company. And a dying man deserves dat."

These last words Miss May repeats emphatically. Folded into the hem of everything she says is a longing for home, the old place, the old ways, the neighbours caring for neighbours.

As I prepare to leave Miss May crumples $20 into my hand.

"Take it," she says. "I know what it is to work and it's wort sometin'."

I tell her I'm insulted so that she has to take it back. She gives me a box of tea biscuits and I'm obliged to accept. It's never good to cross one of the Wise Ones.

MONTREAL: LES MISÉRABLES

Capitaine Nos Nos

My heart stops. The man on the sidewalk has chocolate brown eyes and I fall into them.

"*Comment ça va, ma belle?*" he asks, grinning. How are

you, beautiful? Our laughter touches. I'm being conned.

The east end of rue Ste-Catherine is a gauntlet of bikers, punks, drunks, skinheads, runaways and hookers—a Dickensian world of petty crimes and rivalries. This is the street animal that lives in the night of every major city. More bark than bite. My friend holds out his hand.

"*As-tu des sous?*" Do you have some change?

Pourquoi?

"For a beer. It's hot and I'm thirsty."

His honesty's disarming and we both know it. I give him $2 and a smoke. Teen-agers hover nearby, watchful but keeping their distance. They're waiting for his cue. "*J'te trouve belle*"—I find you beautiful, he says.

"*Arrête donc,*" I tell him. Cut it out. Of the 250,000 Canadians who will find themselves homeless sometime in the year, only in Montreal do they court with such vigour.

His name is Capitaine Nos Nos and my grandmother would be afraid of someone looking like him—swarthy, stubbled, wearing a purple kerchief around his head and a spider-web tattoo on his face. "*La folie de la jeunesse*"—the folly of youth, he tells me regretfully. A bag of dried noodles dangles from his belt loop. All his possessions are heaped against a brick wall: a backpack, sleeping bag, tent, Coleman stove. A couple of teen-agers approach and he gives them my $2 to buy smokes. Capitaine Nos Nos is the unofficial protector of a gang of runaways.

"*Nous sommes* Peace and Love," he says empathically, separating his group from all the others competing for sidewalk. "We take care of each other. And we're not racists like the skinheads. They fight and upset the tourists, then the cops come down on our heads." After hunger, cops are their worst scourge.

"*Sont des chiens,*" Capitaine tells me: they're dogs. "They take our beer and pour it out just to be mean. Or they give us tickets for panhandling knowing we can't pay them. I been in jail twice."

Capitaine Nos Nos and the kids are chronically homeless. The size and shape of their tribe changes according to the season. There are fewer winter runaways than summer ones. Sometimes they squat in abandoned buildings near the Radio Canada building. In the summer they camp in Parc Viger.

I follow Capitaine and a few kids across the traffic into the sliver of a boulevard behind City Hall. This is their home, a patch of grass behind a flower bed on a noisy downtown street. *"Bienvenue chez nous,"* he says, leading me with mock gallantry through the grounds. He leaps suddenly into the begonias. "The garden"—he shouts, then, hanging from a tree —"the miniature forest. And over here"—he waves me to the waterfall—"our laundry and toilet facilities!"

Under the park lights we put up Capitaine's small tent. Seven people will sleep in it tonight. Sixteen-year-old Sandy wants to crash right away. She's cranky and sick with a cold. Sandy's a voyageur—a vacationer. She only lives on the streets in the summer, leaving behind her poor, single mother. She can't articulate why and there's a profound sadness and vacancy to her. Sandy brushes her teeth in the waterfall before going to bed. It's such a little kid thing to do, an act of innocence in this hungry place.

Capitaine and his crew sit in the dark sharing philosophies and cigarettes. Some of the kids are entangled in each other's arms, others are alone. Pasty-faced Patrick claims he's sixteen and looks like twelve. He had his sneakers stolen by some skinheads today and Capitaine promises to get him another pair. It doesn't matter that there's less than $8 among all of them. Capitaine's word is good and the gang lives by it.

The kids wear lots of denim, leather, rings and chains. Their ears and noses are pierced and they look fierce. But they're children: scared, self-conscious, well mannered and easily hurt by adult rejection. Big, bearish Eric with his half-shaved head is more afraid of me than I could ever be of him. He looks at his work boots, listening, but not talking or daring to ask for a smoke.

Bertrand hides behind granny sunglasses, even in the dark. With his knotty stack of hair and sleeveless T-shirt he looks boyish, not tough. Bertrand believes in paganism and reincarnation and claims to remember his past lives. Nobody challenges him. It's an incomplete philosophy, part superhero comics, part charismatic Catholicism, part new-age pop culture. In the spray of psychobabble and borrowed ideologies emerges a tentative code of conduct and a moral through-line.

"Drugs are disgusting," Bertrand says. "And junkies are really disgusting too."

"We don't use violence either," Capitaine Nos Nos chimes in. "Lots of us are already coming from bad scenes. And violence brings the cops. We don't let it happen."

The kids nod in unison. "*Le vol c'est mauvais aussi*"— stealing's just as bad, Patrick mumbles. "We hardly have anything anyway."

Suddenly a couple of male hookers appear, dropping off a few empty bottles for the kids to cash. "*Voilà, les enfants*"—there you go, children. "*Merci*," everyone yells back.

Capitaine sits cross-legged on the wet grass, smoking my cigarettes. He brushes against my leg, arm, trying to put his head in my lap. He wants affection, attention. He needs to talk to an adult. These kids are half his age.

"*Je déjà cherché du travail, tu sais*"—I have looked for work, you know. "I've even embarrassed myself knocking door to door at farms and in the city." He won't ask for welfare—the last time he tried he was turned down because he didn't have an address.

One by one the kids disappear into the tent for the night. Capitaine doesn't sleep. My visit has opened old wounds. When the children are dreaming and the streets are silent, Capitaine offers me his real name like a gift: Alain. His father was Indian, his mother French. He was put up for adoption when he was two.

"*Je suis un orphelin*"—I'm an orphan, he tells me, tasting the words for what seems the first time. Other words come out in a gush: the lonely childhood, the twenty-two foster homes, the running away at fifteen, the years of wandering, the rootlessness, the aching aloneness. He whispers his dream to me of living in the country, on a farm, with a wife and children.

I hold Alain in my arms and he cries deeply, with relief. We rock back and forth on the ground. He smells me, inhaling my history and femaleness. "*Tu me réveilles*"—you wake me up. I smile and pull away. I'm attracted to a man who doesn't live anywhere, who may not eat today. I envy his weightlessness but not his wounds. I wish I could give him more of myself. The withholding makes me feel prudish and English and old.

"*Est-ce que je peux faire le voyage avec toi?*"—can I travel with you? he asks gently. He wants me to share my journey, to lend him my English so he can understand the rest of the country. "*Y a rien pour moi ici*"—there's nothing for me here.

Just before dawn we embrace a last time. Capitaine lingers at the corner of rue St-Denis as I drive away. I can't imagine him as an old man. I turn the corner and cry in my car, and this is what I wonder:

What happens if Capitaine's decency turns sour and rage swallows him? What happens when his street kids grow up and

find themselves so different from the society around them?
Unskilled, unschooled, unwanted. And what will become of
their children?

Already we are Balkanizing. Already there is rage on the
sidewalks, acts of revenge and hate. Do we want people giving
up and flinging their bodies at our feet, our homes, our precious
order? The cops can't save us. The prison system doesn't. The
food banks and soup kitchens only postpone the inevitable. It is
Capitaine Nos Nos who holds back the hordes. And he's weak-
ening.

ONTARIO

Nowhere else in the country do I see such a gap between rich
and poor, haves and have-nots. Ontario is a province of insistent success. It's also the province hardest hit by this latest
depression. Sixty-four per cent of Canada's job losses are in
Ontario—more than 300,000 positions since 1990.

But people still come here to make their fortunes and plant
their dreams. It is a province of strangers: over 50 per cent of
Canada's immigrants and refugees reside here, creating an eth-
nic diversity unparalleled in the country. Ontario also attracts
Canadians from other provinces. They come for the jobs, the
opportunities, leaving their communities behind and putting
down new roots—a little alone, a little intimidated. There are
reasons to be uneasy: the factory jobs are disappearing, and
already over a million people are on welfare.

Ontario is suburban affluence and squalid inner-city rooms
and housing projects. It is small town, fruit belt and bush. It's a
great place to succeed in. And an unforgiving place to fall down
on your luck.

CAPITAL OFFENCES

Ottawa's the same old lady I left years ago, fussing with her plumage and status as capital city. And she's as complicitous as a Victorian about trying to keep the poor and the hired help out of sight. The poor live deeply in the shadows, unnoticed by the tourists and officials who walk by blithely. Ottawa has ripped out slums and built over low-income communities with quiet consistency. She's allowed developers into parts of Lower Town so the poor can't afford to live there any more. She's bulldozed homes and left neighbourhoods lunar and uninhabited—wastelands of memories and good-byes.

It's a town of deliberate and hurtful contradictions. In the Byward Market, where the bureaucrats lunch, an old vet in a wheelchair plays harmonica for change. A few blocks north, a runaway girl sells herself to a man in a car with diplomatic plates. In the park across from the National Library two Native men sleep off the night before. On Parliament Hill a child with a body too thin in clothes too small cries over an empty bottle of juice his mother can't afford to refill. Men in suits look on with disdain. Nothing's changed in my hometown.

OTTAWA: INVISIBLE

I grew up in the west end of fat city and I catch myself driving there instinctively. I follow the filthy Ottawa River through suburbia to Britannia Beach. The projects my most passionate and deadbeat boy friends came from are still here. The boys were French and Irish and just plain old white trash. They tried harder than the rich boys—they had to to get my attention. They were better lovers and better liars. Who knows where they

Lionel

landed, but I look at their homes nostalgically, aching for the confinement of that small world. Funny how some poor neighbourhoods just keep getting handed down to the next generation of have-nots. These rows of townhouses have now been inherited by new Canadians. I watch them walking the beach, the gaggles of Indian girls in saris, dark-eyed Iranian men in crisp shirts and black pants, Chinese families bending around their grandmothers. All at the bottom of the heap like we were, trying to work their way out.

As I sit musing, an old man shuffles quietly in and out of view. He's strangely translucent in his beiges and blues, emitting a soft light. His jeans are threadbare, his shirt a little shabby, but he wears a quiet dignity as he picks through the garbage bins.

Lionel is at peace with his work, not at all hurried or ashamed, unstung by the looks around him. He's got an economy of movement, an expertise that comes from practice. First he stirs the contents of each bin with a stick, listening for cans. He scoops out the prizes with the sharp end and crushes them under his shoe so they're easier to carry. They're worth ten cents each and he never gets his hands dirty. Every few minutes Lionel stops and listens to the idling engines of the city buses nearby. He seems reassured.

Do you like buses, I ask him, surprised by his milky eyes. He's one of the deinstitutionalized, that wandering urban tribe of lost souls.

"*Oui*," he answers flatly. "*J'ane passe de* old man. I know *toute des* numbers. Everyting." He recites a litany of bus routes and schedules to Baseline Road, the Rideau Centre, St. Laurent. It's the sound of an ordered mind in a disordered world, an attempt at sanity.

I ask him if he enjoys talking to people on the bus. He tenses. "*Oui, d'temps en temps*. When dey want. *Mais* I never—I never bug dem. You don't disturb de people or dere's trouble." Lionel is suddenly defensive, accused, insisting on his innocence. "I only talk if dey want, I don't bug dem." We move on to another bin. "I don't bug dem," he repeats.

These are his mind's scars, the warnings branded into his subconscious, an institutional leash. He's grown old around this command: Do not disturb the public. These are official words and they come out in English. Feelings and memories are all French. But the hospital was lived in English.

"Dat's where dey put you if you don't got work."

Where, Lionel?

"Brockville." The asylum in Brockville! That's the place parents threatened to send their naughty children when I was growing up. Lionel doesn't flinch with the stigma.

"I was dere many years. *En a cause* dat I dint 'ave no work. Dey give me *des drogues* and watch me steady. I moved to le nursing 'ome dere four years ago."

Lionel stops and pokes his arm into the bin, pulling out an

almost full can of ginger ale. He offers it to me. I decline.

"I never got de shock," Lionel continues. "But dey put me on des pills. And on de Ward B. *C'est des maudits* screamers, les tough guys. Scream, fight, punch you . . . ." Lionel puts his fist in the air, jerking with suddenly violent gestures. Then he laughs, showing a toothless grin. "Des doctors, dey stole all my years."

Are you angry?

Lionel smiles ruefully. "I used to be hangry but hangry give you fits and fits dey don't like and dey push you arder. Watch you steady."

I offer Lionel a ride to his home. He finds it a difficult choice: his precious buses or conversation. We drive to a streetful of small apartment blocks. Forty-three ex-psychiatric patients share the home. On this muggy afternoon most of them are crammed on the asphalt driveway, trying to get a little breeze. Some sit in clusters, some deliberately, resolutely alone. It's a privately run home, shamefully rundown, with secrets spilling grotesquely out of the bedrooms and into the dark halls. I lose a pack of smokes to the expert cadging of the residents. Their faces are less benign than Lionel's, contorted with medication and disease. Clothing is mismatched, bellies are swollen with drugs, fingers are stained with nicotine. Some are determinedly silent, others jabber their fictions. Too many want a piece of me. An old bent man wants me to register him at the hairdressing school he went to forty years ago. A younger, fat man asks if I know his cousin's children in Toronto—he doesn't remember their names. Lionel walks through them like he's walking on water, with grace and obliviousness. None of them hooks his eyes like they do mine. He no longer hears the screaming or the hysterical sobbing coming from the second floor.

The nervous staff know only the bare bones of each client's

history. They think Lionel might be sixty-six. They don't even know how long he lived in Brockville or what his illness is. Perhaps there never was an illness, just a punishment for being poor or different. Maybe the illness was temporary and there was no other home to go to. But the years of confinement have terrorized and misshapen Lionel, making him afraid to even speak on his beloved buses. Nor did the institutions ever teach him to read or write in those lost years. "It's de source of lots of trouble," he tells me wistfully. "I know my alphabet but I can't put dem togeder." He has memorized his bus routes and numbers.

Lionel insistently gives me a tour of the place. He's showing me off quietly, discreetly. To have a visitor is to be remembered and alive. For a few moments Lionel is envied by his housemates, risen from the dead.

The place is dismal: long and dark with bare light bulbs in the narrow halls. The bedroom doors are open, revealing sleeping, rocking, staring residents. Lionel's bedroom is shared by three. His bed is squished in the middle. There's no private space. Just a particle-board dresser and his shoes and hats stuffed underneath. But it offers a certain freedom. "Here dey don't watch you steady. And de curfew, it's good. But de food, it's not good all de time."

Lionel is dawdling, enjoying my questions and interest. I can't imagine when the last time was he had a visitor to show around. But the place makes me terribly sad. It's just basic warehousing, a business created out of misery and desperation. The company gets a big chunk of each resident's welfare or disability cheque. The clients get a roof over their heads, three meals, and very little more. Almost 60,000 old and disabled Ontarians live in private nursing homes. Too many care facilities are like this, barely meeting basic health and safety standards.

Lionel wants me to drive him downtown. He likes going to the Rideau Centre to sit on benches and look at people. As I stop to let him out, he bashfully reaches into his bag and holds out an unopened can of Coke for me.

TORONTO: THROUGH A CHILD'S EYES

Jesse

Living in Regent Park
by Jesse, age 10

Regent park is a good & bad place for kids. for kids who are knot bad. But there is alot of crack in are area which is bad but they don't bug us. We lived here for 10 years. I have alot of friends who live in Regent park. in the day crack heads don't come out and at night they do come out. And there is a lot of thing to do like go to the Boys's and Girl's club.

Regent Park sits like a canker on the downtown, an inner-city slum several blocks wide. It's the target for lurid crime headlines and campaigning politicians. A place where other people come to build their sociology careers. It's Canada's first and oldest housing project, a labyrinth of mostly low-rise apartment buildings and row houses that are home for 10,000 people. I carry my own prejudice and alertness, watching for trouble, looking for signs, trying to shake off my nervousness. I imagine guns and hate and unpredictable rage—someone yelling at me to get the fuck out. I forget how human nature orders itself, reacting instead like a reader of too many tabloids.

The edges of the park are full of the familiar—dollar stores, pawn shops, hamburger joints, laundromats. The poor fill the sidewalks: battalions of old men in wheelchairs, drunks, punks, single moms, old people with swollen legs, bad-fitting teeth and hair nets. There are the chronic poor and the new arrivals: closed-off Asian faces, hurt black ones. Children are everywhere.

Parliament Street is the dividing line between Toronto and Regent Park. Here's where innocence is supposed to end. But my little friend Jesse sees the world from the inside out. "I'm not allowed to cross Parliament without a grown-up," he tells me warily. "My mom says it's dangerous." What a delicious irony— Toronto as the menace, Regent Park as safety.

Ten-year-old Jesse is a freckle-faced boy with deep blue eyes and long lashes. There's a slight tension in his body, a built-up energy. He fidgets constantly, his hands crawling up his sleeves like ants. "See over there, that's Pigeon Park. Just a buncha drunks," he points out dismissively. It holds no danger for him. "See that store? That's where I go to clean off their shelves."

Jesse is part entrepreneur, part good neighbour, with an unselfconscious sweetness. He spends a lot of time at the Boys' and Girls' Club, organizing hot dog sales and fund-raisers, entertaining the smaller kids and leading litter brigades. There's a staff of locals he looks up to, people to help him grow straight. Jesse used to have a knot of hurt and frustration inside him—a need to hit and swear. Now, he says, "I'm tryin' not to get angry and be bad. And I'm tryin' not to spit. Me and my friend Martin got a deal. One of us spits we have to pay the other five cents. It's workin'!"

Jesse's lived in Regent Park all his life with his mom and dad and his two sisters. He knows the park's contours and mood swings intuitively, steering clear of its rages like a child ducks a drunk father's punch. He's also aware of the area's bad reputation. "I guess there's lots of crime and drugs, but if you don't bug 'em they don't bug you. Sometimes the crackheads try to trip me on the stairs and I just tell my mom. She gets 'em out. What they're doing's bad 'cause us kids smell in that stuff. But I like this area. I wouldn't want to move. I know everyone in my building."

How do people get poor, I ask him.

"They spend money on bingo or don't do right at work and get fired. Or maybe there's no jobs for them. I don't think it's a bad thing 'cause you can help each other. I was selling chocolate bars and I seen this old man on the street and I gave him my tips 'cause he needed it. It was about $2 and he said no. But I gave it to him and I ran away."

Jesse pauses, considering something. "I guess we're poor," he says, wrinkling his eyebrows. "But it's okay."

Jesse's eager to show me Regent Park. Through his eyes it's a wonderful place for kids, village-like and safe. "There's the ball park where we play," he points. "And over there's the swimming pool and basketball court. Oh, and the kick-boxing club."

The grass is littered with paper and trash, but it's easy not to see that when you're a kid. Jesse races ahead and climbs a small hill. "This is where we toboggan in the winter. It's my favourite place of all." We stand together in the wind for a minute, enjoying the view.

"See over there. That's the church where you can get free bikes to borrow." "Do you go to church?" I ask. "Sometimes. My mom never made me go. I just like it. That one at the corner's just for gymnastic shows and funerals. The one across the street's a Catholic one for praying."

As we climb down the hill and manoeuvre through the crowds of kids, I realize that I'm not afraid of this place any more. People know each other here. Kids play together and parents nod to one another as they do in small villages. In broad daylight it could be any of the many towns I visited in Newfoundland. There's a casualness, but also a quiet formality that exists between residents, a shared sense of place. Except perhaps for some of the new arrivals stuck in their foreign languages. They seem more uneasy, more afraid. They heard the horror stories before they even got here. And they keep their children close to them, sometimes inside, all day long.

All over the acres of Regent Park are clubs and social groups, self-help centres and day cares. Residents here are joiners, good neighbours. These mothers and fathers feed the hungry, ignored children of crackheads. They shut down the crackhouses with a quiet courage only the cops notice. I don't see that kind of participation on the other side of Parliament Street, that pride of place.

"Nothin's ever happened bad except for some guys chasing me. I just tell my mom," Jesse says. "I don't talk to strangers. And don't get into cars. My mom and I got rules. I'm not supposed to go out Saturdays until I clean up my room. I do chores like helping babysit, do dishes, clean. I don't get no allowance. I'm grown up so I should be responsible.

"You'd like my mom. She's really neat."

She surely must be.

NORTH YORK: COUNTRYLESS

It is the law of nature that immigrants and newcomers must begin at the beginning of a country, at the bottom. It's the journey most of our families made; generations later we look back and wonder at the folklore. Only dimly do we perceive the compromised dreams and weary lives that fertilized us.

Now it's our turn to decide how many newcomers should be let in. They come anyway, planting their hopes here. Many get ahead, but others spend a lifetime at our mercy, just a set of hands, cheap labour. Whatever happened to our empathy, or at least our manners? Why can't we see ourselves in the faces of these new arrivals? Why do we forget what we learned on our grandmother's knee? "Thou shalt love the stranger as thyself; for ye were strangers in the land of Egypt" (Leviticus 19:34). Once again I enter that other Canada where the disposable people live.

Althea no longer thinks on such things as fairness or good and bad. Her mind has stopped pondering and sits dully in itself. All day she rides the Toronto subway, waiting for her cousins to return from work and let her in. They don't allow her in the house when they're not there, and Althea has nowhere else to go. These are her distant relations, the lucky ones who landed here with all the proper papers. She didn't grow up with them in Trinidad. She's the country girl, the uncle's child, the illegal to be talked down to and bossed. Now they're mad at her for quitting the nursing home job and landing on their doorstep. But it was terrible work: seven days a week, twenty-four hours a day, for $700 a month. The boss even deducted taxes, which of course went straight into his pocket. "I seen some, ohhhh, bad tings. Worst a dem and de worst a me."

Althea's waiting for Saturday so she can begin circling the want ads for nanny jobs. She's an expert in good first impressions: polite, soft-spoken, personable. Pushing down the patois, enunciating in Canadaspeak: "Good morning. I understand you're interested in a capable, qualified nanny for your children. May I introduce myself . . ."

Some days she spends over $10 feeding quarters to the pay phones, talking close into the receiver so the potential employer doesn't hear the street sounds and think she's rootless. Sometimes it's all she can do to stop herself from cussing them for their arrogant tone. She has to put up with it.

"Mummy died when I was ten," she says vaguely. "My fadder was a hard man, drinking, sent me from relation to relation. I came here because dere was nowhere to go. You could say I don't got even a country." It was five years ago that Althea came to Canada as a visitor. She was only supposed to stay three months. Now she's twenty-five, living underground and working the shit jobs for the low pay nobody else wants. She's a deep black woman, thin, muscular. She looks like Tracy Chapman: short hair, hurt, alert eyes. A broad, bright laugh when she's marvelling at people's souls, always forgiving when she shouldn't. She's too smart to be a nanny, and the women who employ her know that. It makes them cautious, fearful, exacting.

"Dere's always a whole set a problems. Dey're nice at de beginnin', wantin' to look smart an' fair. When I tell dem I got no papers, dey got to talk to de husband and den dey come back wantin' to give me two or tree hundred dollar less in pay. Dem say dey're takin' a chance. I got no choice.

"I always live in, I don't 'ave no place. I'm dere on weekends and den it starts. 'Oh, Althea, could you watch de kids a coupla hours.' 'Oh, Althea, we got friends comin'. Can you cook and serve?' See? Dat all what happens in domestic work." She shrugs.

Fast food and service jobs are a lot better. But she needs two or three at a time to afford an apartment. And there's the trouble with fake identification. "I bought a social insurance number from my friend but I don't know where it come from, if dat person alive or dead or waitin' to catch me. I give up using it after a year and a half."

Some jobs she can work at for months without papers, just stalling the boss with excuses. "I tell 'em I jus' moved, or my tings got lost, or dere's trouble home. Like dat." But there's not ever any chance of advancement, no getting ahead.

"I was workin' Harvey's and de boss dere want to make me floor supervisor. But he needed I give him more papers. Every time a boss do me a favour by promoting me is an injustice he's doing witout even knowing it. I got a transfer out to Richmond Hill so I could just keep on as a regular worker. But it always catch up on me."

Althea's eyes brighten as she remembers the good times at the airport cleaning job. "Dat job was boom, perfect," she says, sucking her teeth loudly. "Near six monts, good money. We were workin' in the cargo area. Security started gettin' tight and we had to get a pass from the RCMP. And me, I can't go nowhere near cops. So I ended up quittin' de job. And he was holdin' my pay. So I go to my relations' house and I called him pretendin' to be my own auntie. I talked real nice to him, explaining dat de papers were back home in Nova Scotia. He bought it all and I come back and get my cheque." Althea laughs out loud at the meagre victory of it.

"Den it was back to domestic and babysittin' in Richmond Hill. Dat woman put de baby right in my room. I look after it day and night. Small money too: $550 a mont. I didn't last dere no more 'an tree monts. Dat's when I got de nursin' home job.

"Come on, let's get some air."

Althea climbs up the subway stairs and we sit on a bench in the downtown heat. She feels safe in the swirl of faces and anonymity. Unseen. She relaxes.

"Canada, it have a lot of people play by de rules, but lots of people gettin' away wit lots of crap. Maybe dey're good inside, but dey want to be saving dollars on me. De cleaning job man I called up last week? Already pullin' on me de first interview. Says he's divorcin' his wife an needin' company. Part of me feel sorry for him. And de udder one, wantin' me to babysit his child. Wants to know I got a boy friend and all about my sex life. Personal tings. Dose are de kinds of jobs. But I'm quick. I just move outa de way when de trouble come down.

"You know what I was doing a couple months back? I was so frustrated in de nursing home I wanted to write Oprah. And I started. I got her phone number, in Chicago dere, and I heard her voice on the answering machine. I don't know what I was going to say to her. Right now nuttin's taking root in my mind. Like de old people say, I got no pot to piss in and no window to trow it outa. I'm jus driftin', like a bubble. All I hear from my relations is, 'Someting wrong with you, someting wrong with you.' Someting *is* wrong with me. My daddy usta tie me to a tree an beat me. I only look at him a funny way and he boof me and me feel embarrassed. I got licks, you know the licks I get? Look at my legs."

Althea pulls up the leg of her jeans. Puckered welts as wide as a belt cover the skin. Jesus. I want to hold her, hug her, take away the hurt. If I touch her she will cry. Althea sucks the air between her teeth, making a low whistle, and then pulls her pant leg back down.

"Dey call me aggressive. Lippy. Maybe I am. But I seen how some of de Island girls are, what dey put up with, de guys pullin' on dem, slap dem up at a party, talk to dem anyhow, make dem cry and dem kind of ting. Nobody can do dat to me. Not in dis lifetime. Not anyhow. Bad attitude dey say I got. I can't make dat right.

"Am I soundin' too sorry for myself? Don't be sorry for me. You know what? Soap operas is what makes my day. I take solace in dat, *Another World*, and *Santa Barbara*. I cried when dey took it off.

"I learn good words from soap operas. I got my dictionary and when I don't understand de word, I go look it up. Last week I learnt one. 'Incorrigible.' That was from *The Young and the Restless*. Victor and Jack were arguin' and Victor called him an incorrigible fool. I like to talk nice, and I can."

We fall into an easy silence, the two of us sitting together on the sidewalk. Slowly Althea's face wrinkles in a smile and she begins to laugh. "You ever dream of winning the lottery?" she asks, not waiting for an answer.

"Ohh, I tink of dat almost every day. I gonna make sure to get myself a little house so I have a home for once in my life. And I don't got to be knockin' here an' dere. And after dat, all the money will be donated to charities for de homeless and aids research, dat's what I will do. And adopt a lot a children. You tink dat's mad? And lots a pets too. See dem dogs in dat place, dat pet place, them dogs crying? I'd like ten or fifteen puppies."

WALLACEBURG: THE PICKERS

It's good to get free of Toronto. I need the subtlety of other places, other landscapes. I round Lake Ontario and head south-west into the fruit and Bible Belt. The land stretches out, tidied and tamed by the Dutch, Belgian and German Canadians who farm here. Billboards alert my soul to possibility: "2 miles left. Jesus died for you."

The rain's made everything late this year and there are many worried faces along the way. Farmers cluck and shake their heads, repeating their words of small comfort: "If it were easy, everyone'd be doing it."

Migrant workers fill these fields with bent backs and hot sweat. Some come from the Caribbean and Mexico, and I see their dark faces squinting at my easy freedom. A dwindling few come from Quebec, the remnants of a long tradition of migrants following the whiff of work across North America. Ghislain and his family are from the Gaspé. They've been coming to the fields for five years, and this summer they bring twenty-eight rela-tives with them. For the whole season they're crammed into the compound in back of the owner's place, sharing a trailer home and a clapboard house.

I meet Ghislain's wife crossing the yard with a basket of wet laundry. I know her intuitively: the fire in the eyes, the angry intelligence. Diane's a short, athletic bottle-blonde with a hard exterior of hurt. She hates the work, the dirt, maybe me. We watch each other through the camouflage of innocuous banter. The clothesline separates us like a demilitarized zone. Diane's prickly with exhaustion. She's annoyed by my younger age, by her own worn and leathery face. Where did her beauty go? Poverty's so much crueler to women's faces. It's the women who carry the children and the worry longer into the night, who work and clean and hold up the men until their faces fall off and they wake up old one morning. The smart ones fight being poor, cursing and stiffening under other people's judgements. They kill the vulnerability within themselves as if that were the enemy and hold their fists to the world, demanding a kindness, an acknowledgement that doesn't come. The world turns away from an angry bitch. Poverty can make intelligent women bitter and tough. But they were tender once and raised their babies and worked their love to the bone.

I move cautiously around Diane, knowing her rage, certain of her intent to wound. She pretends not to care and hurries away. She and her sisters are taking a carload of girls to bingo. It's Saturday night and the women have polished their dreams all week.

Ghislain is far less fierce and invites me into the trailer. It's the recreational hub for the whole extended family and a crowd of teen-agers battle over the TV: *Star Trek* or wrestling. The boys are monosyllabic and slouch in their chairs, sucking their smokes to the filters. The girls provoke them out of their mute-ness with ridicule and jabs to the ribs. Ghislain sits alone at the kitchen table enjoying the mayhem. He's a tall, delicate man, gaunt and haunted like a doomed poet, with a thin dark moustache and sparkling eyes. I can't imagine him picking fields. He must run on willpower alone.

"We all work and share de chores," he tells me softly. "Except my girl Brigitte. She don't do no picking, don't like it, so she make dinner and do de dishes."

Picking is hard, dirty work that hurts the back, thighs, knees and hands. Most Canadians won't do it. Pickers are out by dawn or just after, and they work until noon, keeping out of the hottest sun. But this year's rain has kept the crop small. There's been too much waiting around, not enough picking and making money.

"A good day we can make $60 or maybe $75 on de tomatoes," Ghislain explains. But he can't make that on pickles. Cucumbers are thorny things that have to be searched for under bunches of prickly vines. Slow hands make slow money— there's no salary here, you get paid for what you pick. Whatever price the buyer pays, it gets split fifty-fifty between the farmer and the picker.

"De farmer okay, he makes someting, but he put someting in. Seeds, fertilizer, he got to pay for de land. But when you tink what de pickle people get paid, it really makes you sick. Maybe I make $1.77 for a basket of pickles. Maybe de company makes fifteen bottles of pickles wit dat. Dey sell it at de store for $30, $40. It's like de Mafia. Not democracy."

Ontario farmers grew $600 million of produce in 1992. But free trade is flooding the market with cheap imports. And the processors and canners who buy the produce are moving south for cheaper labour. Ghislain fears the NAFTA agreement will gobble up even more agricultural jobs.

He shrugs, smiling with infinite sadness and understanding. The game is so loaded, so stacked against the poor. He knows it. "What can you do?" He retaliates with a few nickel-and-dime scams. He cheats a couple of extra weeks of UI by doing some under-the-table work while collecting. And he pockets the train fare the government gives him to get to the farm, driving the family down in their pickup. These are petty larcenies, white lies. It's not a way of life as much as a substitute for regular, decent work. There are few new jobs in the Gaspé. "De young people are leaving for anywhere else. What we got now it's de ghost town wit just old people."

After picking these crops, Ghislain will go home not

knowing if there'll be any wood-cutting work for him this fall. "Dey talk about free trade, dat's a joke. Dere's no free trade between provinces, so what's de point? I used to work in de bush in Nouveau Brunswick, den dey told us a couple of years ago not to come back, we were not welcome dere. Dey said only de New Brunswickers could work. Bullshit. I tink if we are living in Canada, we can work where we want. Dat's what it is to be a country. And me, I am a Canadian."

The teen-agers turn suddenly quiet, looking uneasily at Ghislain. Some are scowling. They don't feel Canadian the way he does. They feel like poor Quebecers doing dirt work, ashamed to be working with their hands, ashamed to have to leave home for employment. They blame Ottawa for not having jobs. They feel as foreign here as the Mexican pickers, not at all equal partners in some remote federal family. The kids don't believe that this hard work pays off, or pays enough. They don't want to be coming here in ten, twenty years with their kids. Their appetites are bigger, their expectations grander than the last generation's. Ghislain knows this too.

"Me, I'm gonna vote *non* in de referendum. It's nuttin' about English or French like for de young people. De real problem, it's jobs. If de provinces are only for demselves, dere won't be no helping or sharing. It's like too many kids fighting. I want Ottawa to make sure everybody plays de same game, 'ave de same rules and get de same jobs. Dat's it. De rest it's just politics and 'ate."

THUNDER BAY: WAYNE'S WORLD

I'd forgotten how the West begins in Thunder Bay: the wide streets, drunk Indians, drunk whites, the publicness of hope and disappointment. It's the frontier, individualistic and emphatically male. Men drive around in old pickups that don't have mufflers, blaring country and rock music, honking at women in bouffant hairdos. The women stare back, coldly or coyly, depending on the make of man and truck.

It's just to the north of town I find Wayne's place. I can't miss it: a huge heap of metal and car parts and three snarling junkyard dogs. I pull in and Wayne sidles up, looking over my car with contempt and pity.

"They sure make a lotta plastic junk-buckets nowadays." He smiles a shit-eating smile.

What is this place, I inquire.

"Who's asking?" he retorts.

"Well, I'm not Revenue Canada."

Wayne cocks his head and silently scrutinizes me. "Had this on the go maybe ten years. Strictly a hobby." He emphasizes the last word wryly, watching to see if I catch his drift. "Gotta be careful who I let in here. Tax people and government creep around and like to say I'm running a business."

Are you?

Wayne smiles. "Hobby can earn ya a few dollars. I got maybe sixty cars here. I know what I got and people come in lookin' fer parts. Damned recession, I sell cheap and still people can't pay some 'a the time."

This has not been a banner year—he wasn't called back to the gravel pit where he'd worked the last few years driving loaders. And he hurt his thumb in a motorcycle accident. He's living off his insurance. "Don't need much to get by on. And I sure as hell'd never go on welfare. Too easy a thing to get on and hard to pull clear of. I like being free. Mind you," he says confidentially, "now I got this disability from the insurance, I'm gonna milk 'er dry."

Aren't you afraid of your premiums going up?

"They will anyway," he says matter-of-factly.

Wayne's a small man, fortyish, with a rugged brown face and a tight mouth puckered around bad-fitting dentures. He's got a sloppy, floppy looseness: the tongues of his work boots hang out, his shirt tail trails and his square hands are unapologetically black with grease. He's second-generation Finnish, the whole area is, Lutheran too.

"As if that matters any," Wayne chuckles. "Canadian's Canadian."

"And Martian is Martian." Plump, blonde Sheila pokes her nose out of an old pickup. "Ya hear 'ow some people lead and others follow down the path of life? Well, Wayne takes the scenic tour," she says disparagingly. Sheila's the ex-girlfriend. And still in love.

"We lived together a year," she tells me. "We're still friends and all, but I had to get outa here and do something with my life. I mean, look at this place."

Wayne bought the land from his mom. His father ran a gas station here in better times. All that's left is a blistered grey garage at the side of the yard. Somewhere else in the clutter is a broken-down clapboard house.

"Come on, I'll show you," Sheila coaxes me, as if she were still living here. Wayne just shrugs, knowing he can't argue with *two* women. He goes back to banging a door on an old pickup.

The house is decorated in classic testosterone: plywood floors, wood stove heating, dirty tools nailed to the wall. My husband dreams of living like this, shucking off the civilizing influences of women and diving into the dark stink of his own flatulence and primitivism. But he could never get this bad.

Wayne's place welcomes like a garage. It's curtainless and smells of axle-grease, the kitchen has no cupboards, the stove is a Coleman, the oven mitts are a pair of leather work gloves and the counters are crowded with dishes and engine parts. Sheila draws me into a female conspiracy of smug disdain: "Can you see why I left?"

We step back outside and I marvel at Wayne's small appetite for comfort: a shelf full of Louis L'Amour novels and a small black-and-white TV.

"People just want too much. I learned lean living from my dad. I like L'Amour 'cause I can read him straight through and get the story. None of them flowers or poetry. He's clear. And I like *Star Trek* 'cause it's the way we're going."

"See what I mean," Sheila says, shaking her head. "The scenic tour."

"D'ya tell her I got no indoor shitter?" Wayne asks, deliberately embarrassing Sheila. "Go look at it."

I cross the yard to Wayne's outhouse. Inside, the floor is littered with hundreds of discarded toilet paper tubes. He's smirking when I return. "Cozy, huh?"

Wayne is a man unlined by worry. He works slowly at his pickup, banging the reluctant door onto the cab, enjoying the long days of talk and chores and visitors dropping in for parts.

"You been following this constitutional circus?" he asks, not waiting for an answer. "Fuck 'em all in Ottawa. Those clowns don't know a thing about unity. Freeing up trade with the U.S. and we can't even open up our own provinces. Settin' one part of the country against the other. Jobs is what would keep us together."

"What do you know about it?" Sheila asks. "You can't get along with nobody."

"Can too. So long's they don't try movin' in."

"I don't want to move in. No one does." She looks at me. "He was married once. Lasted *five months!*"

"I like the way I live. And that means alone. You come around and I can't find nothing."

"Yeah, but you, in all this mess, you can't find nothin' either," Sheila continues. "I'm not even livin' with you any more and you call me up askin' me where your insurance papers are."

I slip away quietly, hardly noticed by either of them.

"Nice to have met you," Sheila calls. "Good knowing ya," Wayne nods.

Then they resume their positions at each other's throats.

THE PRAIRIES

This is the forgotten country, a place between places, a place between time. It's a land of farmers and natives, of wide spaces and cramped cities, the agricultural heartland.

The highest rates of child poverty in the country occur here: 26 per cent in Manitoba, 21 per cent in Saskatchewan. A severe pride lives here too, and a stubbornness. But eighteen-hour days on the land can't muscle away weather and hostile markets. Farmers are hanging on by their fingernails. Despair inches into their hearts. People are leaving, selling, going bankrupt. In Saskatchewan there's a joke about it: "Tell whoever leaves last to switch off the lights."

MANITOBA

It is late summer as I cross Manitoba. The poplar trees are already turning yellow and their leaves twist delicately like weak-wristed old ladies. It makes me sad. I think of Gramma.

I pass through many strange-named towns: Dugald, Gimli, Hochfeld, Napinka. Manitoba's population claims the highest non-British and French ancestry in the country, almost 50 per cent. Waves of immigrants came from Germany, the Ukraine and Iceland, building their churches and towns.

The province is full of old history and unfinished business. More Indians and Metis live here and in Saskatchewan than anywhere else. But they still live at the edges, on the streets, disappearing into wounds from the last century.

WINNIPEG: THE TOWNSHIPS

Oh, Jesus. Winnipeg hurts the eyes. It's easy to miss the obscene living conditions if you're on the tourist trail and keep to the imposing shadows of the downtown monuments. It's easy not to notice the 40,000 Natives who live or wander on these north-end streets. But just cross the invisible barrier and you'll be embarrassed by the Native township called North Winnipeg. Here are the cheap hotels and rooming houses, the barely adolescent hookers, the glue sniffers and Lysol drinkers, the flophouses where three generations of the same family will come to sleep, the piss-stinking phone booths with a heap of broken human inside. This is what Canada looks like to many Prairie Indians.

One of the wounded corners of the north end is Logan. It runs along the CP main-line tracks. Ten years ago the city axed Logan to pieces, expropriating houses for a commercial park that existed only on paper. There were no tenants or proper financing, but poor people were pushed out of their homes. The city even rezoned the area as commercial, preventing residents from getting building permits to spruce up their properties. But the community mobilized, standing up against the city and grabbing its neighbourhood back. Civic pride was restored and now there's a community-run school, a newspaper—and unde-

niable spirit. But the poverty and hurt don't disappear over-
night. I stop at the Logan House Community Centre and find a
small, dark-haired director named Lori. She rages and laughs at
the contradictions of the place.

"We've got a social worker for every fifteen people living
here, either a public-health nurse, welfare worker, parole offi-
cer, juvie worker. It's a fucking growth industry. They're
getting jobs while people around here stay as poor as ever. So
get rid of it, just pull down the whole system. Send everyone
a cheque—guaranteed annual income—and just get rid of the
weight.

"The only time we get the mainstream press down here is
when we have a murder or rape or when something else horrible happens. What nobody ever notices is what's well here,
what's functional. It's the sick stuff they come here to see. It
confirms something in them about poor people, something
about their moral superiority. But it kills *us*. The image we see of
ourselves is ugly and cruel and distorted and scary. It makes
our children ashamed.

"If you really want to know how poor people make it work,
go see Vera. She's the backbone of Logan."

LOGAN: MOONYACQUE — THE GOOD WHITE WOMAN

Vera runs the local food bank. She's sixty-six years old and she
couldn't give a good goddamn if her teeth are in or out. Nor
does she much mind how she looks in her tight pink T-shirt and
her green stretch pants. "I never wanted nothing for myself,"
she says proudly. "Never wanted jewellery, watches, pretty
dresses. Always wore slacks 'cause my arse felt bare in a dress.

Jessica Lee *(left)* and Vera

Never even wanted dishes. I got 'em all mismatched from the Goodwill."

Vera raised fifteen of her own children and hundreds of foster kids, alone and sometimes on welfare. There wasn't time or money for self-indulgence. And there isn't now. "I got forty-four grandchildren and fourteen great-grandchildren, including Jessica. I adopted her when she was two and a half."

Jessica's a bright, saucy ten-year-old, mercilessly dragging her cat by the tail. "Leave it go, Jessica Lee," Vera hollers. Jessica doesn't pay any notice. "Talking to kids is like talking to the barn door," Vera mutters. She grabs Jessica by the sweater and gives her a smack on the rear end.

"We're too scareda our kids nowadays. Can't hit 'em or yell at 'em without it being called abuse. Bullshit. I gave mine a few good whacks and for the most part they've turned out good. You want some tea?"

I laugh, enjoying Vera's moral certainty. She's of the same

tribe of women who mothered me—strong, tough and unequiv-
ocal about right and wrong. I miss their parental guiltlessness,
the absence of self-doubt. How they yelled so freely in the
Miracle Mart, their voices freezing me in mid-crime. Or their
shameless habit of hitting publicly, whack!, on the side of the
head in the parking lot. Yes, there are small wounds—a slight
lowering of self-esteem, a nervousness about authority. What I
gained was moral clarity and generous civility. I see these traits
in many poor people: good manners and eagerness to please.
Fierce mothering is one of the strongest civilizing forces of the
poor, the root of pride and place. It's one of the things I am most
grateful for in my life. I like Vera right away.

Vera's home is small and sparely furnished, in the lower level of
a house owned by Manitoba Housing. It's crawling with babies
and toddlers, grandchildren who Vera minds during the week.
She wades through them easily.

"I love kids. Had my own and hundreds of unofficial ones
the nuns from Rossbrook sent me. My kids brought 'em home
off the street too. Sometimes we didn't even have mattresses for
them. And I still got my own coming in looking for something.
Usually food or money!" Vera laughs, shaking her head. Her
oldest girl, Eileen, is in the living room waiting for me to leave.
"She wants to borrow money," Vera says caustically. "But she
won't ask in front of you. So stay as long as you want."

It's a noisy house with lots of surprises. Vera bends with the
fates or just ignores them. "That's my boy Reed." She points to
the man coming in the door. "He works the food bank with me.
And that's his wife, Claudette. Face as long as a wet week."

"Hey, Reed, you remember when we usta dig fer seneca
root?"

"Yeah, Ma . . ."

"We'd go into the bush while my older boy Ronnie minded the other kids. There was a big market for it in France; they put it in castor oil. We sold it to the Hudson's Bay Company. Made $2.65 a pound for it. We'd wear potato bags slung round our shoulders. Made $30, $40. Enough for groceries."

Vera is white and the Natives who respect her call her "Moonyacque": good white woman. Her parents came from England to farm in Manitoba. Vera had to quit school in grade five because the family couldn't afford the books. She grew up near a reserve.

"I always said when I was a girl I wanted to live with the Indians. My mother read us Indian stories, stuff about Samuel de Champlain. I met my first husband, Robert, on the Lake Manitoba reserve. I lived there twenty-three years. We had kids and then we split up. He was a good man but not when he drank. His mother died drinking antifreeze. We were together eight years.

"Then I lived common law with Walter till 1976. We had ten kids but he was drinking and beating on me. My old man was a great hunter, I have to say, but the drinking and beatings, it was no good. He even had a rifle to my head. I don't know how that old bugger's still alive. He worked on and off at odd jobs those years, nothing steady. But as long as there was food and my kids had clothes, I didn't give a hoot.

"Now I don't allow any drinking in my house. And nobody's allowed in drunk neither. Not even Christmas. They want to do their drinking, they do it outside. I don't need any more of that, now do I?"

Vera sucks in her breath and watches intently as her youngest daughter saunters in looking for detergent. "She steals something bad, that one," Vera whispers. "Pawned my vacuum cleaner. It hurts, but it's not a life, it's just a thing. I hide stuff when she's around. Gotta have eyes in my arse."

When Vera left her second husband she moved to Winnipeg with her ten youngest children. "I had to go on welfare. I never cheated and I never asked for more. They wanted to give me money for Jessica but I said no. I got my pension and we live on that. At least one of my kids won't be raised on welfare."

Not that welfare was ever enough. Vera kept a garden and canned her food. She got charity from the Sisters of Zion and occasional bags of groceries from her father. She stops for a moment, remembering his kindness. It makes her sad. "He always wanted to give us more than he could." And of course there was meat when her boys hunted.

"We always shared our food with friends and neighbours. And I can still carry a hind quarter of deer on my back down the basement stairs." Vera's one of the few in the area who still remembers how to cut a deer and dress it. "They don't know how, that's the God's truth," she says incredulously. "So I get meat outa doing it for them."

Vera has a talent for getting by. It was her trading and handiwork that kept her children warm and filled their mouths. And left few moments for personal pleasures. "I always lived poor and kept clear of bingo every night. I had my sewing—I love sewing. And my Wilf Carter records. I tried bingo a coupla times, even won $280 once. Forgot to yell bingo. I yelled, 'Oh fuck.' But if ya can't afford it, then go without. My Ronnie, he says you only live once. I says yer a fool.

"Being poor's all right. It's how you accept things. Neighbours, other ways. I got along good. I just let the wind blow. But if I run low on food I'm a regular bitch.

"I'm lucky. My kids turned out pretty good. I got five married, the rest common law like me, married but not churched. But I won't lie for 'em. I won't turn 'em in either, that's up to the cops to catch 'em. You do the crime, you do the time. Only one of my boys been in real trouble. Another one stole a semi and he had to pay a $500 fine. I wouldn't pay fer him. Ronnie got him a job at the optical plant, and he paid it up. The good Lord's been good to me."

You religious?

"No way. I don't go for that Sunday stuff, not my cup of tea. But there's someone there and it don't matter to Him where I go to believe in Him."

Vera suddenly roars across the kitchen.

"Jessica you put yer shoes on if you're goin' outside!"

"Yes'm, master," Jessica yells back.

"Don't be cocky with me or you'll get a hot ass."

Jessica makes a face but holds her tongue.

"Poor's a different way to live but I think poor people are hurting more now," Vera continues. "TV makes them hungry for things. And not working makes 'em sick inside. Look what they done to the Indians.

"It's the damned government's responsible fer makin' us dependent. In '58 there was *no* welfare. I remember it well. It was a bad winter, lots of snow. Before that winter we had pride. We were hard working. Now the reserves are killin' us. Reserves usta be safer than the city. My kids never swore till I came to the city. Now it's worse. It's a sad place. Old and young used to pick berries, smoke meat. Not now.

"You know there's no word for please in Ojibwa. We never had to beg. We didn't steal, either. Everyone was welcome to everybody's things. If someone had nothing, you gave what you had because one day you'd have nothing. Now you got chiefs and band councils stealin' from their own people and everybody waitin' fer cheque day."

Vera moves effortlessly between the two cultures. She speaks Ojibwa fluently and raised her kids in it, but the city children pushed it aside for English. She's taught the language as a volunteer at the local school. And her son Ronnie, who works at the cultural centre, often calls home to find out the meaning of Ojibwa words. Vera has a remarkable gift for seeing both the beauty and the artifice in people. She doesn't much notice exterior details: skin colour, accent, language, religion.

"I can't stand prejudice. And I'd like to know where it comes from. I try to get along with everybody. The people next door are from the Philippines. They give me some of their Chinese food and me and Jessica give 'em strawberries. They're hardworking people in sewing factories. They'd do anything. I like that about people."

"You ever eat elk?" Vera serves up plates of meat and onions, boiled potatoes, white bread and her own pickled beets. And there's bannock, too—a flat, cake-like bread brought by the Scots. It's spirit food, good for dreaming. We wash it down with Kool-Aid. I ask Vera if there's anything she missed and wishes for in life, any regrets.

"None. Life was bad, some people say, but I laugh now. It wasn't life let me down. The bottle let me down. Life gave me lots of good times. Oh, we used to love wrasslin', me an' all the kids. I can still throw Reed on the floor. And the hose fights! Bring the water hose right into the house. And perfume fights too. I had a lot of laughs all the way along."

We stand at the door for our good-byes and Vera gives me a great big bear hug, almost lifting me off my feet. "So what else can we bullshit about?" she cackles. I leave feeling I've left one of my mothers behind.

ST. AMBROISE: OLD DREAMS

I've often heard of sacred grounds and magical places where old bones speak, of cultures that believe in such things. I've imagined them more in Ireland than on the Prairies, but here by Lake Manitoba the land is haunted. And I inadvertently sleep on it.

I drive tiredly into a small, birch-lined provincial park at Clandeboye Bay, wanting only rest and some time alone. It's Friday night, Labour Day weekend; the wind picks up and howls all night, dragging in grey wet skies.

I'm terribly lonely tonight. Little families rumble past in the dark and I miss my Liam and my husband. I settle into a damp tent and dream strangely. Somewhere in my deep sleep I hear a voice: *"Qu'est-que tu fais là, Daniel?"*—what are you doing there, Daniel? It's a deep voice, disturbing, and I become vaguely aware that it comes from outside me. I want to stop the dream, but I can't. Deep, deep, deeper I go, lost to myself. Gone. Dimly, I become aware of rushing footsteps. People are moving on either side of my tent, running, and I can tell by their sounds that they're crouching as they run, hiding, pursued. I see flashes of orange light as small pots of fire are carried past my tent.

I'm fighting to get out of my dream, to surface, and as I near the border between night and light, I realize that I'm no longer dreaming. These people are real and they're running away in great panic from something terrible. Slaughter.

I'm terrified now, and I try pulling myself awake, but I can't get up off the ground. I try to make a sound, to scream, to will myself back to myself. Then a huge rumbling, a gagged roar, comes out of my belly and into my mouth, propelling me awake.

"Daniel," the voice bellows. Not my voice. And I lie awake in my sleeping bag, scared stupid. The footsteps outside my tent, the people, are moving away. Their noise and vibrations are fainter, hardly perceptible now. I lie in the dark very afraid but still sleepy, as though I'm being pulled back into the dream. I don't want to go back, I have to stay awake. So I throw off the sleeping bag and slap myself with the suddenly cold air. Who in the hell were they? Indians, I'm sure. Sioux. I remember something vaguely—their crouching, their hair, their long faces. Definitely Sioux. I'm awake now, trying to make sense of senselessness. Could it be that elk I ate at Vera's?

I scramble to my car and lie rigid in the back seat, waiting for dawn. Whose bones have I been sleeping on? What is this place? St. Ambroise, French, Lake Manitoba. Must be Metis. Perhaps these are Metis spirits. Who is Daniel?

Morning doesn't come early enough.

ST. AMBROISE: BEFRIENDED

Just after dawn a maintenance truck rumbles slowly into the park. I hurry alongside, coming eyeball to eyeball with a Sioux face, one from my dreams, hook nosed and thin lipped. Beside the driver sits a squatter, darker man. They stop the truck.

"Good morning," says the driver, curious at my early wakefulness.

"Who's Daniel?" I blurt out. The men exchange quizzical looks. I continue, feeling stupid. Unable to shut myself up. "Was there ever a battle around here? Maybe between Indians? I had a strange dream last night."

"What number were ya in?" the Sioux-faced man asks.

"Twenty-one."

"Yeah," the other one answers knowingly.

Yeah what? Yeah, there's a Daniel? Yeah, I'm crazy? Or

yeah, twenty-one is a cemetery full of Indian bones? Their in-scrutability is unnerving.

"This is Sioux Pass Marsh," the driver tells me. "Sioux came up here an' tried to push the Metis into the lake and they got pushed right back. Ran like rabbits all along the shore. Died too. Daniel's probably my great-grandfather: Daniel Ducharme. First Metis settler around here."

Both men nod at me in unison. They believe in dreams as firmly as they believe in anything else.

"You wanna come back to the office with us? Could tell you some of the history. I'm Paul, this's my friend Georges." Georges grins a little too eagerly, but at least there's no ridicule.

I follow them into the concrete innards of the park repair shop. A couple of other men are there too, Metis, warming themselves with coffee. "Lady here had a dream about the Sioux last night," Paul says as a way of introducing me.

"Hmmm," is the general reply.

The men are all dark, Indian-looking. Bleary-eyed this early in the morning. Paul's a quiet, twinkling man, satisfied and wise. His cousin Ralph's a lot rounder, more playful. Georges has got a strong French accent and a hung-over, brooding look. They're all in their midfifties, relaxed in themselves and without sharp hungers. Except Georges. He continues to watch me.

"The Cree and Metis got together to fight off the Sioux," Ralph begins to explain. But Georges interrupts.

"De come trough from Nort Dakota after de Battle of Little Big 'orn. Dey fought two weeks and de Sioux were pushed back to Sandy Lake and Erickson Mountain. You got kids?"

"That was in the late 1870s," Paul interjects quickly. "The Sioux dug themselves in here, waitin' fer the Cree and Metis."

"I'm a widower," Georges cuts in. "My wife died five monts ago. My kids are grown up. How 'bout choo?"

"That was pretty hard going for Georges," Paul adds softly. Georges bows his head in exaggerated sorrow.

"Maybe it's time ya found another one," Ralph winks. "A young one." Everybody laughs, then they look at me.

"You wanted to know about Daniel? My great-grandfather came here from Quebec," Paul continues. "Came through Churchill and down the Nelson to Lake Winnipeg."

"Where's your family from?" Ralph asks. I tell him Ontario, Ireland, Quebec. His eyes light up. So do Georges's.

There's a round of smiles as we begin speaking in both languages. "So you know about Louis?" Ralph asks. Louis Riel. These guys speak about him and Gabriel Dumont as if they were neighbours, as if they died last week. They argue over where Riel's bones are. Ralph thinks they're in Regina. "No, dat's where dey hung him," Georges disagrees. "Then Batoche?"

"No, that's where Gabriel is," Paul insists. "Louis's in St. Boniface, Gabriel's at Batoche," Georges says with finality. Having settled their histories one more time, the friends gulp down their coffee and turn to thoughts of work.

This is the last official weekend of summer and these jobs are seasonal. Winter begins next week and so does the uncertainty about employment. "These're good jobs here for Natural Resources," Ralph clucks. "Four months of sure work. June to September."

"And dere's de goose and duck camps for de Americans. Dat's till November freeze-up. We're de guides." Georges cocks his head sideways, trying to impress me. "We make good money. Sometimes $800 or $1000 a week."

There's also ice fishing, what the people here call hook fishing. "The best little hooker on Lake Manitoba. That's what they call my wife." Paul chuckles. The pay's so bad there aren't enough people willing to do it. A lot of wives get roped in—up at dawn, work till dark for $40 a day.

"It's not so bad," Ralph says, unconvincingly.

Georges sighs. "Me, I'd get out if I could," he whispers. "But dere's nowhere else to go."

ON THE GREYHOUND

The wild flapping and zigzagging of tourists is ending and a kind of bleakness settles into the silence. This weekend marks the end of summer, and people are buttoning up against the cold and heading back home.

I take a bus from Winnipeg to Regina along with a crowd of poor young Torontonians. They're on their way west looking for work. They fill the back seats with loud obscenities and cigarette smoke. Twice the bus driver threatens to kick them off. They're cocky, but when a mother asks them to watch her sleeping child so she can slip into the bathroom, they are as sweet and obliging as their mothers raised them to be. None of these boy-men has anything waiting for him at the end of the trip except hope and a few relatives. Twenty-year-old Adam is going to introduce himself and three of his friends to an aunt and uncle he's never seen. His plan is to get construction work in Vancouver.

Across the aisle, a lanky twenty-three-year-old German student is folded awkwardly into the small seat with a philosophy book. Occasionally he watches Canada through the window. As we talk, I'm struck by how educated and sophisticated he seems compared to the young Canadians. He has a quiet confidence even though his future is as uncertain as the other kids'. Robert's a poor man's son: his father's a factory worker, his mother a house cleaner. But there's a definiteness of culture about him, a sense of membership and ownership. What is the difference? Perhaps it's education. Close to 27 per cent of fifteen- to nineteen-year-olds in Canada drop out of school each year. For poor children, the rate is 45 per cent.

SASKATCHEWAN

There's a slow, terrible drowning as autumn brings wetness to the plains. Less than a quarter of the crop has been cut by the time I pass through, and the wheat's the lowest grade in ten years. Farmers combine all night in a race against the frost. Many will lose.

Saskatchewan's the only province in the country to have lost population in the last five years. There are fewer than a million people living in this huge, empty space. I spend hours driving between places and seeing no one, achingly alone except for the sting of wind and sky. It's a land of narrow conversations. Hope, love, laughter are conveyed silently, with small nods. But you can't farm on dust or mud. I'm reminded of Newfoundland—a small population surviving on bad weather and natural resources.

I'm surprised how people remember the Dirty Thirties here. They died on this land, for this land, back in the bad times. It was the memory of that suffering that pushed Saskatchewan's Tommy Douglas to create North America's first free hospitalization plan in 1948, a scheme that led to medicare many years later. But what miracle will these new bad times bring the next generation? Surely some good will come. People in Saskatchewan keep looking to the horizon for that.

WEYBURN: POVERTY ACRES

Weyburn is a dumpy, wheezy old place with a weary face that hasn't had cosmetic surgery. Thank God. There are so few of these towns left, unassaulted by the forces of modern developers and American-style malls.

Weyburn is disguised as Crocus in W. O. Mitchell stories, and I meet the wind here, kicking up dust and pushing pop cans down the streets. It fills my heart with ancient awe. What a fierce personality the wind is on the Prairies, up and gone so quickly. Today she's hot enough to fry the eyes in my head. I boot it down Number 13, windows open, air conditioner blasting, hurrying away to some unknown relief. A sign stands out on the side of the road and I screech to a halt: "Poverty Acres."

Typical prairie humour. I have to knock on the door, way up along a dusty road.

The lean fellow who answers has a definite twinkle.

"Why Poverty Acres?" I inquire.

"You hearda the working poor? That's us," comes Len's quick reply. "We gotta both work full time to keep this place going."

Life's contradictions line his face. He's got country-singer good looks and a tight, cautious mouth from thinking and worrying. He leans into his house and hollers to his wife: "Woman's from Toronto, Lois. Wants to know about our farming."

Lois seems amused and invites me in. She's a bit stouter than Len, more settled in herself, with a round, girlish face and the same soft, laughing eyes. We sit drinking Coke as Len darts around with a fly swatter—he can't sit still for long. Lois talks about their two children in high school. Their cozy home sits on three hundred acres of farm land. Everything in sight has Len's handprint on it. It's far from aching poverty, but it could turn into that, and as suddenly as a prairie storm.

"We're slippin' backwards," Len says matter-of-factly. "Grain usta sell $5.80 a bushel ten years back. Now we're getting $2.07. I got two bins full over there, see?" He points to the small red silos. "That's 140 acres—$6000 for a season's work." Lois shakes her head sorrowfully.

"And fuel's up too," he continues. "Maybe to an Easterner a five-cent hike's not much. But it is to us when we're usin' 30,000 litres a year.

"We're not puttin' our money into all-new equipment the way people say we're doing. I'm farmin' with junk. My newest tractor's from 1962."

"And we use my dad's combine," Lois adds. "We got three of us families using it, and then we do his combining for him in exchange."

Len and Lois have the same prickliness I've seen all over the country as people watch themselves in the mirror they think Central Canada is holding up to them. "We're not lazy," Len insists. "Most of us aren't stupid. Some of us might want too much in the way of equipment, but we're stuck on our land and we gotta work harder than you think to keep it going."

Len and Lois, like more than half of Saskatchewan's farmers, hold other jobs. Len works installing windows and Lois is a paralegal secretary for a firm that's closing down in a month. Without two incomes, there's the real possibility of sliding into debt. And there'd be no way to crawl out—farm land values have dropped over 40 per cent in the last decade, and wheat's fetching Depression prices. But the off-farm work doesn't allow for many breaks.

"A Sunday off is finishing at 4:00 P.M. insteada after dark,"

Len chuckles. "We work early morning, go to our jobs, then come back and work into the night. The kids help out."

"We usta dream about making the money we pay in taxes now," Lois says jovially. "But in a good year the crops pay for the land, and our jobs pay operatin' expenses. There's nothin' left you'd call profit."

"Taxes, now there's another crock," Len says. "We're the highest-taxed province in the country. Hardly any people still here, so they're shaking the change outa the pockets of the ones left. We've thought of walking, but we're too far in. We'd lose too much."

"Mixed farming's the answer," Lois says with the certainty that comes from many arguments defending this position. "When grain's down you got higher cattle prices. Don't ask me why, but it seems to work out that way. But then you're stuck here, feedin' and grazing. We got no more time for any more chores."

The only choice is to work through this depression and bad weather. And to wait. Like other grain farmers, they can't just take their crops to market. They have to wait till the quotas are announced. Farmers are allowed to sell only a percentage of their crops. Right now it's 2.9 bushels per acre of grade one or two. If you've got a low grade, a three or four because of hail or some other act of God, there's no sale at all.

There are farmers who get stuck with full granaries of low-grade feed grain. But there's a built-in lottery to farming, because grain has a long storage life. Take Lois's father—he suffered through three years when no quotas were called for his grain. He had no choice but to stockpile. He was going broke and hungry. Then finally his grain was in demand and the price shot up and he made some cash. But he could have starved too.

"Hope's the only cheap part of this game," Len says. "We're

hangin' on fer a turnaround. But what'll a world with continental free trade be like? Better days might not mean the same thing as before."

Lois hurries in to fill up the silence. She knows not to tempt bad luck with negative thinking. "All we want's a fair price," she says. "We don't want handouts, and we sure don't want the paperwork that comes with it." Lois is the bookkeeper. She knows the bureaucracy.

"And we shouldn't give our grain away to other countries," Len whispers, swatting a fly on the table. "Sure, I don't want to see people starvin', but what would ya do down East if we gave away every second car you made 'cause you'd made too many or nobody was buying?"

There's something even more fundamental to their thinking than attacking the middle of the country. It's about the future of their children. That brings the biggest ache of all. "We figure it's gonna cost us $12,000 to put our youngest through university," Lois explains. "Where's that money gonna come from? On paper it looks like lots of money comes through here. But not much of it stays. So she can't even get a student loan. Our son wants to go to the agricultural college in Alberta, he wants to farm. But we can't encourage him 'cause it's impossible on this land at this time."

As we say farewell the wind kicks up and the clouds spit out a heavy torrent of rain.

SASKATOON: MOTHERHOOD

There's no use even thinking of going into Eaton's or The Bay. There's no money for those kinds of places. But Sheila's got to buy *something* today, a small extravagance, any little thing: a

Sheila

toy, a T-shirt. A small purchase always lifts the soul and the self-esteem. She marches into Woolworth and rummages through the clutter of the toy department.

Sheila's been out of jail for three weeks, and she's all nerves. In a few days she'll be getting her three boys back and with that comes the hydra-headed Children's Services.

Sheila's been in jail four times for fraud. Altogether, she's served twenty-nine months at Pine Grove Correctional in Prince Albert. Always for bum cheques.

"I know how it happens. I get like this pressure from welfare. Just being on social services is degrading. Nickel and dimin' ya. I get no breaks. Hassling with the fucking workers. So I kinda just bust out." She shrugs, trying to explain the inexplicable rage and helplessness that erupt from deep down. Her face changes when she talks about the system—she screws in her mouth and narrows her eyes. Behind the hardness is a beautiful face: big blue eyes, full lips, the robust good looks of a high-school cheerleader. She's disarmingly angry, funny and vulnerable. She softens most completely when talking about her children.

"Mostly I do it for food or the kids. I write a cheque for a VCR or something, then I go pawn it for groceries. It all depends on what kinda mood I'm in. Depends what we need. My kids don't have nice clothes, but I get lots for them. And I make sure we eat a good meal once a week, meat and potatoes. So I write a cheque for meat. Or I take 'em out for supper." Sheila pauses for a moment, remembering something. She smiles vaguely. "I once wrotta cheque for pictures of the kids at the Sears studio."

I smile to keep from crying. These are the things I want for my child.

"I always feel terrible after writing a cheque 'cause there's no way to turn back," Sheila whispers. "After all the scrimping and not having I just want a little bit of what everybody else has. But it's wrong. I know that."

During her incarceration Sheila's boys are put into the temporary care of Children's Services. "My six-year-old asked me the last time why I was going to jail. He said, 'You're not gonna do that any more, are ya, Mom?' "

Sheila's bottom lip wavers and she sucks in her breath. "That was really hard." She wipes the tears away with her hand. "Those babies weren't put on this earth to suffer. But every time I get a problem with welfare and start fucking up it ends up hurtin' them. I don't mean for that."

Sheila doesn't feel like shopping any more. She leaves Woolworth empty-handed and we walk to a nearby bench. Her voice softens. She wants me to know how hard she's trying. She wants someone, anyone, to acknowledge that.

"I never been out without gettin' a babysitter. Never left those kids alone once, like some others I seen. You can't imagine what it's like not seeing them when I'm in jail. Not knowing

how they're growing, what they're feeling. Being all twisted up
'cause I know it's me doing something to them. I had my last
one, Trevor, in jail. Gave birth to him in there. They took him
away from me. You don't know how much that hurts."

The three children have two different fathers. Neither of
them gives Sheila any steady support. "The oldest one's dad, he
buys Kyle three-piece suits for church, good shoes, even golf
clubs, if you can believe that. But a few months back when we
all got sick, Kyle needed cough syrup. We needed food money.
But not a cent from his dad. And he's got a decent job. The
other one, Ryan and Trevor's dad—guy never kept a job. The
only way to keep him is if I put the son of a bitch on welfare.
No way. Fuck him. With all the time I been in for fraud, I'm
not serving any more time just to keep a man.

"Most of the women in jail are there 'cause they're poor—
bum cheques, beatin' on their social workers. All 'cause they're
poor. I'm not saying poor's an excuse for breaking the law, but
it grinds you down. I don't know what it's like to have new
furniture. Seriously, I'm lucky if I eat once a day when I have all
my kids. There's so little. I pretty well rely on my child tax credit
for my kids' Christmas. And I always end up selling my income
tax. Costs 15 per cent. I know I'm losing, but I need the money
right away."

Sheila lives on $535 in welfare for herself and three children.
She's supposed to get $800 but the Saskatchewan government
docks the amount of her baby bonus as well as grabbing back
monthly sums for overpayments mistakenly sent to recipients
like Sheila. I keep going over the numbers with Sheila, doubting
her calculations. I mean, nobody can live on that. She's patient
with me, and a little amused. "Welfare's just a different kind of
prison. When I'm inside at least I don't worry about eating."

Sheila's not without ambition or a desire to escape her poverty. She tried college before her last child was born, studying computers and accounting. She got a student loan. But she wasn't prepared for the weight of paper, the five hours of homework cutting into her children's time. She had to quit. Now she owes on the loan. And she can't go back for a hairdressing course she wants to take until she's paid up. She's her own worst enemy and she knows it. Her rage is so deep, so impenetrable, she's a problem for the system, the social workers, the officials who are supposed to help her. But it's the rage of intelligence, of self-respect, of frustration. It's the rage of a bruised child.

"My whole family's fucked up. My dad's name was on the docket the same day I went to court last time. He's been in and out of prison, on fraud too. Every time Mom threatened to leave, Dad would buy her a washer or something, then sell it when he got drunk. He drank bad, and when he left, my mom turned alcoholic. I never got into the booze, I don't know why. But I got into the cheques.

"I'm thankful to the justice system. I know that sounds weird but they helped me learn about this so I'm more aware. See, there's a pattern passing on to my kids. I'll show you."

Sheila pulls some paper out of her bag and draws two circles that represent her parents. Around the outer edges she draws a lot of little circles—they're supposed to be her aunts, uncles and grandparents. "See," she says with great earnestness, "there's alcohol and dysfunction in all these people but two. It just kept getting handed down. And it's up to me to break the cycle. See, I understand how it works now. I don't know if I can break the pattern, but it's up to me to try. For my kids."

I listen to Sheila's psychobabble, these blunt tools given to her by the prison system. They seem more capable of cutting her open than cutting through old patterns. What an enormous pressure to bear this half-knowledge, this self-blame. Her optimism is astonishing.

But right now I watch this wounded, unsure mother chain-smoking and trying to convince herself that she can manage the huge and lonely task of mothering three boys by herself. She knows what happens when she can't take the pressure. And she knows what happens if she fails as a mother.

"I been away from them for a while, and I don't have the patience. Sometimes I yell and it bothers me. I got a short fuse till I get usta them."

Suddenly Sheila's mood lightens. The talking has done her good. She drags me to the Army Surplus for another round of bargains. I love the old place: the creaky wood floors, the reluctant elevator, the immigrants and Natives and poor whites who look at the price tags before looking at the merchandise. Sheila takes her time, luxuriating in the plenty, in the possibility.

"Could write a cheque here, I bet," she says teasingly.

We make our way to the kids' section, touching the frilly little-girl dresses.

"I'd love to have another baby, just one more. A little girl," Sheila tells me dreamily. I'll always remember her face at this moment, so full of hope and possibility and second chances.

THE WEST

This is the New Canada, the new affluence—suburb after suburb of shiny homes and realized dreams. The West is a little smug in her abundance: the ethos here is one of self-reliance. Poverty is reviled and considered a scourge from the East. But the poor live here too, more quietly than elsewhere, more cautiously. Many came in the boom years and ended up busted. Others got all the way to suburbia only to lose their jobs. They pay the mortgage but get their groceries from the food bank. They are not so good at being poor, these New Poor, not quite as practiced. They're afraid and secretive. Often they lie to their families about their hard times. Often they have no families, no community to depend on—they pulled up roots to live out the national dream. They are alone, ashamed, sometimes embarrassed about how they used to blame the poor.

The West is on its way to eclipsing the industrial centre of Canada. The poor follow, greasing the economy with cheap wages. Vancouver is choking on its underprivileged and homeless.

The New Canada is not so unlike the old Canada.

ALBERTA

I vaguely notice crossing an invisible line. There's an abrupt affluence at the Alberta border. The pickups are spanking new and shiny. I leave behind Saskatchewan's clunkers, land boats held together with string and spit and prayers.

Albertans are persistently optimistic, whispering their failures only to close friends and family. The homes are generous, the land is good, and there is little of the obvious poverty I've seen in other parts of the country. Even the downtown hookers on Third in Calgary manage to look unscarred and better pressed than anywhere else in the country.

No one should be poor in this land of black gold and honey, but those who are face a hostile public. In another couple of months the province will be led by the same Calgary mayor who once told the "eastern welfare bums" to "git."

CALGARY: MEASURING OURSELVES

Calgary is a flat, beige, suburban sprawl. I enter the hum of it, driving around and around what feels like the same subdivision: rows of detached and semi-detached bungalows, strip malls, Mac's Milk stores, Pizza Huts and Tim Horton doughnut shops. Poverty's been tucked away behind middle-class façades. I sense secrets on the other side of the vertical blinds and fences.

I get to the southeast end, where my oldest school friend lives, desperate for a dose of home, a little comfort. I don't know what Lynda's last name is any more. There have been at least four: maiden, married, an alias to shake off the past, and finally another man's last name from that short, mistaken second marriage.

We go back to elementary school in the west end of Ottawa. Lynda and I met as clumsy arrivals in another suburbia. I remember what a frontier it seemed back then, undeveloped fields of possibility for everybody's fresh start. Homes and schools were going up faster than we had boy friends, and so were class borders. Suburbia was in fact two very separate places, a minefield of subtle disparities as inevitable as human nature.

The newly rich plopped themselves into subdivisions with names like White Haven—and didn't that say it all. These were homes for the downtown merchants, doctors and lawyers: classy two-storey houses with fake Corinthian columns and Grecian pretence. Inside were pianos, wall-to-wall carpeting, intercoms, *luxuries.* No *True Detective* magazines, though. The rich kids were bossy little snots, made arrogant by their slight edge in the world. We accepted their friendship only in the dead heat of summer when we used their pools.

Lynda and I lived in the other suburbia, the bungalows, semi-detacheds and town houses. We didn't have parents on the PTA, or clowns at birthday parties, or summer camp. Our mothers didn't stay at home redecorating our rooms. They worked, along with our fathers, overtime, sometimes at two or three jobs—slaves to the mortgage, buying us the chance they didn't have. Our parents were tired and cranky and worried a lot. But finally in their own homes.

Lynda and I preferred the rougher company of our working-class friends. While the richer kids dawdled in their development, maturing slowly, lingering in their abundance, there was a jitteriness to our growing, a hurry to live. We used our bodies and our fists to claim position and satisfied our itches with booze and drugs, sex and delinquency. Many of our crowd barely made it through high school. Some landed in jail, others in juvenile detention, unskilled jobs. Many rushed to the boom towns of Toronto and Calgary. A lot of the girls had babies young: Sue, Susan, Ellen, Gabby—and Lynda. She was sixteen when she got married, sixteen and a half when her baby was born. She moved into a world of adulthood and postponed pleasures. Our friendship became sporadic.

What a relief it is to see her now; it's been a couple of years. Her sons are men; they're sweet, loving, I can tell. She's a little stouter, with the same dark mop of hair and unmade-up face, the same gap-toothed grin and hug. The same "How th' fuck are ya."

"Doin' a book on poor people," I blurt out.

"Great, came to the right place! Fuckin' economy stinks, politicians breakin' up th' country and seven people on my street tryin' to sell their houses an' can't. Including me. Come on in."

We are instantly ourselves with each other, falling back into our working-class, Ottawa Valley accents. Ooohhh! Nothing can relax my jaw, my soul as much as speaking this first language with someone from home. "You'z all look great!" I hear myself saying.

Poortalk. It's such an ugly thing to some people; a kind of mumbled obscenity, a spray of ungrammatical, chewed-up words, an affront to the finer ear. I know that, we know that, and we've learned to speak the stiff, dried-tongue speak. But among ourselves our talk is wet and gooey and unhurried. The lips are lazy, relaxed, the tongue's uncurled, flat, blunt-bladed, so that words roll out uncut from each other. Sounds are grouped into single statements of sentiment. "How are you doing" becomes "howya-doon."

The real magic of poortalk is what it does to the body, the posture: how it unlocks the shoulders; how the neck and head loosen, the knees come apart and the hands move as freely as birds. Rich people hate it. There's nothing more impudent or insulting to their self-importance than the slouch and casualness of poor people.

Lynda and I both flop on chairs and sprawl our arms out on the kitchen table. We talk in feelings, impressions, anecdotes, blabbing out our heaps of opinions. We listen not for academic merit but for clues to each other's wounds and victories, our state of survival. We move through the house, spreading ourselves over every piece of furniture, filling every ashtray. Finally we stretch out on Lynda's bed with the ease of girls at a pajama party.

"There *are* things make us different," Lynda muses.

"You mean poor people?"

"Yeah."

"Like what?"

"Like we're not usually full of ourselves, for one thing. We love more and we take care of each other. And being poor makes you feel nervous about yerself. We're always worryin' about not fittin' in. But one thing, we're not fucked up about our bodies like they are. I mean, the kids seen me naked all their life. And we been with more guys. All the wrong ones."

We both laugh guiltily.

"And we swear more," she adds. "I've learned not to do it out loud but I do a lot of it in my head. 'You fuckin' peckerhead,' I think when my boss is bein' an asshole."

Lynda thinks poor people are more tolerant and caring. And more honest. She might have a point: 3 per cent of welfare recipients defraud the system, but a quarter of Canadians cheat on their income tax.

"And we're more honest about ourselves, about what's inside. I don't hide things from my kids. They know about my mistakes. About being broke sometimes. Shit, Lindalee, I wasn't jokin' when I said you came to the right place for yer book. We're just hangin' on in this fuckin' recession. I'm rentin' the basement and I'm still barely makin' it."

Lynda's worried. I've never seen her worried.

"Things are bad out here. Lots of people around here counting on two incomes, one loses a job and goes on UI, and they can't pay the mortgage. Just across the street my neighbour got laid off. They're living on her husband's salary: $2400 a month. Their mortgage is $1300 and they got three kids. Secret Santas came at Christmas with donated presents. My neighbour was cryin', she was so happy. But she was humiliated too.

"I figure the fuckin' banks oughta pay fer welfare and helpin' out homeowners through this depression. Bastards been rakin' it in forever and none of it ever comes back to the common good. Social programs should be guaranteed, an' if the feds can't get the money to do it, charge it to th' banks."

CALGARY: THE FOOD BANK

Calgary's media are trying to get a big turnout to the food drive. They're billing it as Fun for the Whole Family: a parade, hay rides, country music. I wince. Lynda is adamant about going.

Canada's first food bank started in Alberta in 1981. Today there are almost 350 of them across the country. More than a million people use them, two-thirds of whom are children.

Lynda heads for the grocery store and buys the stuff she'd like to eat: tuna, fruit salad, cheese, cookies and juice. Forget the Kraft Dinner. She hauls three bags of groceries in her beat-up '77 truck. It's not the kind of splurging she can afford.

Hundreds of families come to the Stampede grounds on this blustery autumn day to share their food and fun. I'm divided in myself. I love the giving part of it, the good intentions, the community effort. But I'm disgusted by it, too. A bag of groceries can't change the causes or course of poverty.

Half the Calgarians who use the Inter-Faith Food Bank are on some form of assistance. Welfare doesn't give them enough money to eat. The other half are the working poor: part-timers and minimum wage earners who still can't feed their families. The issue isn't about food, it's about unemployment, decent wages, fair distribution of wealth, reliable social services.

I watch the well-fed faces moving about the fairgrounds, sturdy in themselves, enjoying the day, while a poor family skulks around the free hot dog counter, suspicious-looking, as if they're up to no good. I can tell by the father's furtive glances, his secretive manner, that he's ashamed. He's not sure whether to ask for a second hot dog for his little girl. Only the poor worry about looking poor; the better-off are lining up three deep for freebies. And so the man stands there hesitantly. His daughter, in a tight, second-hand pink snowsuit, has the anemic ghost-white face and limp hair of poverty. So does his bloated, nervous wife, in her stretch pants that are tearing at the seam. This is what a high-carbohydrate diet does to the human body, what happens when people can't afford protein and vitamins. These are the Kraft Dinner People. Their children are often doomed in the womb, neurologically stunted by malnourishment. Compared to middle-class kids, they suffer twice the rate of psychiatric disorders, twice the rate of poor school performance and chronic health problems.

Lynda and I sit on a bench eating our free hot dogs and

watching the ironies play out around us. She's unusually pensive. "I had to get food from here a few years ago," she tells me
softly.

Lynda the legal secretary? The woman who's always held
two or three jobs and even went back to school? The one who
does tax returns in shopping malls for the extra money for her
boys? I try not to act surprised.

"I was between jobs, it was near Christmas. Everything had
to go to the mortgage. There was nothin' fer food. I thought I
could just pick up the food, so I phoned. They told me I needed
a referral. Thing is, you don't want anyone to know and everybody ends up fuckin' knowin'. I had to get my doctor to call
social services, even though I wasn't even on welfare. Social
services gave me a card and I went down to the food bank, got
in line and all for three bags of groceries."

We hug delicately. I wish I had known. In a couple of
months Lynda will lose her job and slide onto ui. She'll spend
a worried winter hanging on by her fingertips. Maybe she'll
go back to the food bank and not tell me. Why the hell aren't
there enough jobs for all the people like Lynda who want to
work?

BANFF: OF MICE AND MEN

The snow comes early to the mountains, a sudden squall as
heavy and wet as rain. Two shivering teen-agers huddle together on the curb in Banff. One is small, delicate, hungry-look-
ing, intensely intelligent. He smiles at me.

"Are you students?" I ask.

"Not," he says, grinning. "Lookin' for work. Just got in.
We're from Brandon and we're looking for anything."

Jason *(left)* and Dean

He holds out his hand good-manneredly and shakes mine. "I'm Jason. This is my friend Dean."

Dean is a darker, more internal boy of seventeen. He's still growing and has that awkward, stretched-out gangliness. He nods at me and shrinks back into his shoulders, wanting to stay invisible.

"We got a friend coming at lunch time with the keys. She's letting us crash at her place," Jason tells me, shoving his hands in his pockets for warmth. For now they're just waiting and wandering around Banff. "Great town. Good music," Jason enthuses.

"It's like Disneyland. Like someone drew it," Dean mumbles.

They hardly have enough money left to eat—just $20 and a bag of popcorn between them. Dean started out with $250 but he paid for their bus tickets.

"I'd rather starve than go home," he says flatly, unable to fish out his deeper feelings.

"Home's a nice place to visit but I wouldn't like to live there," Jason laughs. "There's no work back there."

"Jason's gonna get us welfare," Dean assures me.

Jason nods. "We gotta get a job first. Then we go to Canmore and they'll give us welfare to hold us over."

"We're gonna make it, no doubt," he assures Dean. "We got to."

"The Banff Springs is hirin'," Dean reminds him.

"It's dirt work," Jason scoffs. "Dish pigging. There's work in the oil camps up in Nelson too. What they say, $1200 every two weeks? But it's really dirty work. Just sleep and work. And there's no place to spend yer money, which I guess is a good thing. But it doesn't stoke me. I wanna learn ballet. Dean, ya got another smoke, please?" Dean digs into his pants pocket, then lights one up. The two boys share it.

"When she say she was comin'?" Dean asks carefully.

"For sure lunch time."

They resume their silence.

Jason's parents are teachers. He wears a middle-class confidence, a cockiness, with a tinge of disdain. This poverty's just a passing thing, something to get through. A lark. Dean's more hesitant. More afraid of being poor. His dad's an orderly, his mom's a cleaning lady.

"I totally didn't want to end up like them, work, work, work," he says from a rage deep down. "My parents want me to finish school. I got my grade nine and I figure nine years is a long time to do the same thing."

"Whole plan's to get us lost in their educational system," Jason says with authority. "It's too easy."

"Maybe we should try those rigs in Nelson," Deans says cautiously.

Jason stares back coolly. "Not."

Jason's friend Susan finally does come, a sisterly girl from home who works in a gift shop. The boys put on their best manners and a genuine show of gratitude. Up in the little apartment, Jason hands Dean a bottle of vitamins with paternal urgency and then swallows some dutifully himself.

"Last time I was here I had nowhere to sleep so I slept in the park. This's a definite improvement," Jason chuckles. "The only thing I miss about not havin' money is drugs."

"We all outa bones [joints]?" Dean mumbles.

"Yeah. But heard there's 'shrooms around. We'll look into it."

Jason pulls out an ironing board and rifles through his bag for a pair of black dress pants. Dean sits in a heap at the kitchen table and watches him ironing.

"This is just a costume," Jason instructs. "People think, 'Hey, that guy's got something going for him.' When I don't have a thing going for me!"

"You do too," Dean insists loyally.

"Yeah, I guess. I believe in being nice. I'll spark a joint and give my last one to anyone. I'm totally outward. I'm a Gemini. The only people I hate are in the KKK. I can't take them beatin' up blacks and gay people. That's sick. I've seen some gay bashers and I've taken 'em down. See, the world's gettin' screwed. Too many issues. My act of personal protest is not voting. All politicians are liars."

"You wanna see my skateboard?" Dean asks me, rousing himself from his silence. He disappears into the next room.

"We spend too much hate on people we think are different," Jason continues. "We could totally have enough if we shared. We got enough food and there'd be no homelessness either.

Instead we're wasting time in our towns worrying about who's makin' more money. I saw a bumper sticker said, 'Whoever has the most toys when they die, wins.' That's it totally."

Dean returns and gently hands me his skateboard. "Man, we had some good times on this," he muses. "When we stopped in Medicine Hat we skateboarded and almost missed the bus."

Jason barely hears him, concentrating on his shirt sleeves and the untangling of his inner knots. "The rich got too much power. I don't want to slag people who worked hard for what they got, but we pay too much attention to the rich, as if they've got, like, something special to say."

Jason holds up his shirt, inspecting it critically. He turns to Dean. "You're not wearing that to look for work, are you?" he chides.

"Yeah. But I'm gonna iron it," Dean mutters defensively.

When his friend leaves the room, Dean bends over the ironing board, scrutinizing the faded creases in his jeans. His big hands move clumsily, trying to match the seams. He looks like he's deciphering Chinese. I press the pants for him.

"Jason's got it all worked out good. But I don't know how to be different." Dean lowers his voice. "I don't have nice enough clothes to fit in around here. These are Woolco specials, that's where we shop at home," he says, pointing at his pants. "I got good shoes, but nothin' else really fits." He looks directly at me for the first time, beseechingly, as though I might have the answer.

Jason returns in his white shirt and black pants and rummages through his duffel bag. He carefully pulls out a folder.

"I brought my résumés," he says proudly. "Gotta make one up for Dean. He didn't even know what they were."

Dean shrugs sheepishly.

"I took off from home last year, then I went back to finish

school," says Jason. "But I couldn't do it. I got my grade eleven and half of twelve. Now I'm prepped to see the world."

"I think people think we're bums sittin' on the street with no job," Dean worries.

"Maybe they do, but I promised myself that I'm never going back to Brandon. I'll sleep on the street if I have to." Dean looks up at Jason sceptically, pulling his arms around himself, as though chilled.

"Come on, Dean, comb yer hair. We'll ask to see the manager at the Banff Springs. Give him our résumés."

Jason walks determinedly into the cold, head first like a boxer going into the ring. Dean follows, dragging his feet and pushing his fists into his pockets.

"Trick is to show them yer neat and keen and easy to get along with," Jason counsels.

Dean's face tightens with apprehension. But he fakes a smile for Jason.

BRITISH COLUMBIA

Ahhh. Eden. Our favourite province of all. The national shift is again westward and the nation is hauling her dreams here. I've been tempted before, and I'm tempted again driving through this splendour. One hundred and thirty-four thousand people have moved to B.C. in the last five years. There is wealth and the illusion of wealth. But there's a quiet industrial collapsing: traditional work in forestry, fishing and mining is shrinking. There's been a 40-per-cent increase in welfare cases in the last few years. Some blame it on the new arrivals. But surely the blame is economic and political.

I meander slowly through the Crowsnest Pass, massaged by the beauty of rocks and sudden lushness. It's just past the coal mines of Fernie that I hear news about the Westray mine in Nova Scotia. Charges are pending against the mine managers there. I wonder how my friends are healing.

CLEARBROOK: FAMILY SECRETS

Bill is lying to everyone. It's a complicated fiction. The welfare office thinks he's unemployed and his working friends think he's got a job. He manoeuvres secretly and expertly through the fraud. But it carries its own weight, and a gutful of guilt. He lives in a row house in a modern, flimsy, low-income project. His home is spotless as a bunkhouse, hushed and full of fear.

"I've always worked, I want you to know that, ma'am," Bill begins defensively. "When I was in school I worked part time in construction, and I pumped gas in the summer. I've done every-thing—I've sold alarm systems, worked restaurants and bars."

His wife, Beth, nods vigorously. She's a thin, blurry pres-ence, whispering in a soft German accent. Trying to disappear into the furthest end of the sofa.

It was a crooked beginning Bill came from—a violent, drunk father, a grade eight education that got him as far as the CN section gang. The military straightened him up, bolstering his confidence and giving him the surest route into membership. He spent seven years in the Canadian Forces—in Laar, Ger-many, and in Cypress as a UN peacekeeper. That time left its indelible markings on his life: he's polite, erect, bristle-haired, though now his trained body is softening with middle age. His T-shirt reads "Support the Forces."

"I enlisted in 1978 as a private," Bill continues, "$19.50 a day. And it was a twenty-four-hour day. I made it up to master corporal. The military's great if you're single, ma'am, but for a family it's a killer."

Bill, his wife and baby daughter headed into civilian life and it was good. The couple managed an apartment building together. It was steady work, and decent paying. "We had a rent-to-own TV, furniture and a $20,000 Suzuki four-wheel drive."

Two years later the building was sold.

"We lost our jobs. And we owed lots on our credit cards. Funny, 'cause we didn't start out wanting credit. We got Visa sent to us and we didn't even apply. Then Canadian Tire, then everything else. We took it all. We ended up owing $35,000 in credit cards and cars.

"We had to move in with her parents and then a series of basement apartments. Her parents thought I was a bum." Beth bites her lip. "The bailiffs and creditors just wouldn't quit, ma'am."

I interrupt. "Please stop calling me ma'am."

We share a smile, then Bill continues.

"I took anything, and I mean anything. I'm not afraid to work. She babysits, and that's legal under welfare. She's allowed to make so much. I paint houses under the table. We never took off and we never went into bankruptcy. Our plan was always to pay off those bastards. It took us these last five years. We got $3000 still owing.

"See, we make $800 a month in welfare. That's not enough even to eat. I don't know how other people do it without cheating. But it's changed my way of seeing things."

There's a silence and an internal accounting as the couple reflect on who they've become and who they used to be.

"We never started out wanting to cheat," Beth says softly.

"But the average Canadian calls people on welfare scum-sucking sons of bitches," Bill says with sudden hardness, pulling himself to the edge of the sofa. "We're making do with sweet screw all. It's spit in a bucket compared to the $11 million Ottawa spent on its own birthday party. Cross my heart, spit to die, sticka needle in my eye. I believe you treat others like you'd like to be treated."

Beth gives Bill a wounded look, as if his rage has betrayed them.

"Look, I'm a real flag-waver, ma'am. I love this country. I swore on oath to die for this country. But we're run by greed now. You see it better from the bottom looking up. We've got doctors here making $300,000 and they're screaming because the B.C. government wants to knock back their pension plans. Is a guy stopping a puck worth $3 million? That's what the goalie for the Vancouver Canucks gets. I mean, what are we rewarding these days? What's of value? Big business sucks off billions in subsidies—look at that Westray mine thing—but let's slam the welfare people."

Bill's steam evaporates and he flops back against the sofa, limp.

"I don't know if we're bad or what," he says softly. "Here I am a thirty-year-old man on social assistance with a wife and daughter, scamming $300 a month. The guilt of doing this is so *uuggghhh!* I've had to deal with my morals, my manhood. You know how it feels to sit with a bunch of employed friends putting down welfare bums and just havin' to keep quiet? Or thinkin' I could get my ass hauled into jail for what I've done?"

Bill goes to get himself a glass of water, retreating into a necessary silence. Beth smiles, a little embarrassed.

"Nobody knows. This is all a secret," she tells me. "Our four-year-old daughter doesn't understand, thank God. We

could use a boarder here, but we're too afraid to bring someone
in. They could tell on us."

"Adapt and improvise. We learned that in basic training,"
Bill shouts from the kitchen. "And that's what I been doing for
the last five years. Maybe I am a scum-sucking loser, but my
little girl won't know any of this. We're going to make it!"

His words hurt Beth, making her world wobbly. She can't
bear to see her husband's aching. Her love for him is obvious
and protective. She turns to me. "Do you think what we're
doing is wrong? Are you going to write that?"

It's a plea more than a question. I look back into her ordi-
nary face—there's nothing sinister there, nothing diabolical or
evil. It's the kind of face that gets lost in a mall crowd or a
church picnic. I tell her I don't know what I'd do if all that bad
luck fell on top of me. I tell her I know there are different sets of
rules for different circumstances. But her crimes seem so pathetic to me, so necessary. And their fear leaks into every part of
their lives. For what? All they want to do is honour their obliga-
tions. Who the hell am I to judge?

VANCOUVER: INDULGENCES

There is only $23 in my bank account when I arrive in Vancou-
ver. There's a certain symmetry to it, I suppose. I've lived these
last six days on credit cards—I buy smokes at gas stations where
they accept credit, meals at department store restaurants where
I can use a card. I've been cadging food and beds at the houses
of friends. My one relief is knowing *my* poverty is temporary.

But it still carries a feeling of inferiority. I'm afraid of being
found out, of one of my cards being spat out, of having someone
behind me in the bank line sniff when my request is rejected by

the bank machine. I imagine everyone knows I've only got a few bucks left, that I'll be judged harshly, treated poorly, dismissed. Poverty makes me feel so small.

My appetites are huge, suppressed. I march into The Bay on Granville and put a few extravagant items on my charge card there. Perfume for me, a bagful of toys for my son, who I won't see for another two weeks. I feel relieved, valuable, less marginalized, a part of the consuming classes. A citizen again. Afterward I feel sickened by the indulgence. Weak. Ridiculous.

VANCOUVER: DUMPSTER DIVING

Gary *(left)* and Jonene

It's a damp, discouraging night, Vancouver's version of autumn. Only the poor and the homeless are unhurried, staring out like cats from bus shelters and doorways. But there's a beauty, too. The wet pavement bleeds with reflected light, making the city almost festive. Even in the alleyways there's a vague kind of warmth and cheer. Jonene points it out to me.

"Don't you think it's kinda pretty?"

Her boy friend, Gary, doesn't agree.

"I think it's kinda wet."

The two of them are out on their nightly round of garbage picking—dumpster diving. It's a perfect time for it. The drizzle keeps away most of the competition, and only a couple of other determined scavengers push by us with shopping carts.

Jonene and I dawdle as Gary walks ahead of us. He's a hefty, greying man in a ski jacket and baggy pants, intent on the task ahead. He bangs the dumpsters expertly, listening for the weight of their contents.

Jonene's daintier and more excitable. She's in her late forties but elfin-faced and girlish. "I guess people would call us a couple of lowlifes," Jonene chuckles. "It took me a while to get used to doing this. But it helps us out and we get some wonderful things."

This is central Vancouver—Kim Campbell's riding—and it's a place of contradictions. All along Robson Street the poor and insane collide with rich yuppies and smartly dressed gays. At its back side, the neighbourhood contrasts are stark and Third World. The luxury condos are gorgeous and lush gardens cascade like Rapunzel's hair. But there are miles of fortifications and wrought-iron gating. Even some of the garbage is locked up. Where there's disparity, there are fences.

The alleyways cut through the neighbourhood like the Green Line, a demilitarized zone between urban tribes, where the poor come to feed. It's always full of eyes and travellers. The building dwellers look down at us from the yellow light of their warm homes. Gary and Jonene don't return their stares.

"Got something," Gary murmurs, waving his flashlight into

the black pit of the dumpster. We all stand on tiptoe and peer in. He fishes out a cushion with the end of his coat hanger.

"Whaddaya think?" he asks Jonene.

Jonene inspects it carefully.

"Probably sell. But look . . ."

Jonene spots a green garbage bag spilling with clothes. She's partial to fashion, always looking for something for herself. That annoys Gary. They're supposed to be looking for things for their daily garage sale. Every morning they haul their acquisitions down to the sidewalk on Bute Street, elbowing a space among the drugged and mentally ill vendors. Residents eye them suspiciously. But the couple earn an uneasy peace through an exaggerated politeness. They're both on disability. The rent gobbles up more than half their income, so the garage sales pay for food and other necessities.

"This could be great pajamas," she says, holding up a pink sweatshirt. "Look, there's another bag down there." Gary sighs but dutifully pulls it up for her to look at. Jonene rips it open and yanks out a couple of shirts for Gary. She stuffs them into her plastic bag.

We keep walking and I feel my self-consciousness disappearing. There's a certain freedom, a kind of invincibility when you can live through hostile stares. Not even the gawking children in the BMW disturb us. Ours is a childlike logic: don't look at them and they can't see us. We walk in our own invisibility, enjoying our ghost time.

Jonene and I are giddy as Saturday shoppers, chatting nonstop as Gary silently trots ahead. There are many false hopes, many disappointments as he pulls things out of the dumpster and throws them back. The antique lamp has lost its plug. The portable TV has no guts. The futon is too heavy to carry.

"Look, Gary, I always wanted an espresso machine." Jonene

lingers at the pile of trash. The appliance box is empty, but just looking is good enough.

Jonene met Gary outside the liquor store. "He was playing his guitar there. He was really nice," she chirps.

"That was the best spot in town," Gary reminds her. "I worked eight years there and good money."

"But he had to sell his guitar," she says with finality.

"For forty-five bucks." Gary winces, remembering the low price. "I used to teach music at the conservatory in Toronto. Came out here and wrecked my back."

Jonene used to be a social worker. "Funny, eh? I mean, to look at me now. I had over two hundred cases back then. Used to pinch food vouchers to hand out to my clients. I couldn't stand seeing them so poor."

She got disillusioned and moved to other work. Then a back injury put her on disability too. Still, there's no bitterness in her. Just a little wistfulness. She and Gary have managed to work out a satisfying business for themselves. And they've kept their appetites simple.

But tonight the rain won't let up and they're soaked right through—they head home. It was a lousy night. But Jonene's got her clothes and Gary's hauling a couple of plastic stacking crates back with them. It'll have to do.

Seven months later a druggie has a skirmish with a local and the cops swoop down and push the vendors out of the area. Jonene and Gary have to find someplace else to sell their wares.

ROBERTS CREEK: THANKSGIVING

Cheryl calls her old car "The Beast." It's a 1980 four-door Plymouth Volare. She lives in it.

Cheryl

I meet her on the tangled edge of the Sunshine Coast. The Beast is idling and Cheryl's doing her nails. "Wanna see my house?" she laughs, yanking open the passenger door. The interior is strewn with the typical possessions of a twenty-year-old: guitar, small stereo, make-up.

"I'll show you my basement," she says, pulling open the trunk. Her clothes are neatly organized in separate plastic bags: underwear in one, outerwear in another. Her wardrobe is almost completely colourless.

"I'm just comin' out of a black phase. I spent three years just wearing black. It was definitely weird. Hiding my hands up in my sleeves and just basically disappearing. Now I'm totally into Celtic stuff. It's harsh. I got this put on—see?" She shows me the tattoo on her right forearm. It's a Celtic braid etched right around her arm.

She smiles proudly, an open-faced girl, sweet and guileless, not at all hard.

"This yer first time in the Creek?"

Yep.

"The Creek's a totally cool place. You can count on people. You wanna drive around?"

It is a child I hear in her voice, someone small and alone. On this drizzly, chilly Thanksgiving Sunday neither of us has anywhere special to go. We curl into the warmth of The Beast, and Cheryl drives me through her landscape. The coast comes to us vaguely through the wet window, a knotted green place, overgrown and hidden at the edge of the grey Pacific. Cheryl knows every house and all its secrets. Each home is a thread in her safety net, a part of the fabric of herself.

"Creekers are the best. They help out a lot," she enthuses. "They let me take a shower, stay for a few days. We all know each other here.

"I do a lot of house-sitting. That's how I get to stay places. And babysitting too. People around here go away and leave dogs, cats, chickens, even horses. Sometimes they go for a weekend, or even a whole month. I do it for money but a lot of times it's just tradesies. Like I took care of this mechanic's house and he fixed my car.

"But sometimes they come home early, like last night, and then I'm stuck finding a place."

Cheryl would like her own home but there's no money for that right now. She goes to school all day, finishing her grade twelve. She gets $450 a month from welfare to live on. Just enough for school and gas.

"I had a friend's mother fake a lease agreement so I could get that much. I need a place, but something for less than $400, which is totally impossible around here. Winter's gonna be much harder."

She shrugs, pushing away more desperate thoughts.

"Wanna see where I usta live?" Cheryl stops and circles

back, pulling into a dreary trailer park: little skinny boxes on asphalt, no yards, no privacy, just a row of trailers in each other's shadow.

"Wow! I haven't been back here since we left. That used to be our place, there."

It's one of the uglier ones. No flourishes of imagination, no awning or porch or add-ons. Grim. Cheryl disappears inside herself and doesn't look at me when she speaks.

"My dad took off when we were young and my mother had the three of us. We didn't have money for clothes or anything. I went to skating lessons a couple of times but I had to quit 'cause we couldn't afford to buy the skates. Then my mom got this boyfriend. I remember wakin' up one morning and she was gone. My aunt was there. She told me my mom'd gone for a holiday in Florida. That was hard to take."

Cheryl fires up The Beast and drives out of the trailer park silently. "I left home when I was sixteen and moved to Victoria," she tells me when we're safely far away. "It got pretty weird with some of the people I was hanging out with. I lived on the streets a lot in Victoria. Hung out with a tough crowd. One of the guys I was hanging with got charged with murder. And there were fights, really bad ones. I sewed up a guy's hand who was in a knife fight. He didn't have a health card to go to the hospital. He wasn't scared at all. I didn't want to but he yelled at me, 'Just fuckin' do it.' That was the most disgusting thing I ever did, sewing up human skin.

"We used to be really punked up over there. There were three of us used to hang out together. They're still at it, but not me any more. They're totally, like, middle class and I think it's kinda disgusting now. I mean, they spend all this money to look poor and I know what it's like to really be poor. And there isn't anything nice about it."

Cheryl pulled herself off the streets and came back home to the Creek for her grade twelve.

"I gotta laugh. I usta babysit some of the kids I go to school with now. I know I look kinda stupid. But I got a mission to tell the kids not to quit. If I can tell 'em about that and have them listen, that's good enough for me."

Cheryl's future is still a blurry, unknowable place. "I want to do something in the Third World, Somalia, some place like that. I need to help people and I need to get an education so I can do that."

We turn off the road onto a gravel lane and The Beast shudders over the potholes. The Pacific stretches in front of us.

"This is Sandy Beach. I come here a lot when there's no place to go. It's the safest place to crash at night."

We both get out and breathe the wet air.

"You know, the old poorness hurt me," Cheryl sighs. "It was harder. We always worried about money. It made us scared. And we felt little and embarrassed a lot. But this poorness is just something on the way to something else. I'm not really poor. I mean, I'm not poor on the *inside*. I'm learning a lot right now and I'm going to give somethin' back. I got a plan and I guess that's my plan. I don't want to live in my car forever."

NOT FORGETTING

I sink finally, gratefully, into the certainty of home. I'm grabbed back fiercely by my husband and our boy, Liam, and I rest for many days with their arms around me. I crave silence, order. I take many baths, luxuriating in a brief amnesia. But rage can't be scrubbed away.

Over four million Canadians live below the poverty line. That's almost the entire population of countries like Ireland, Kuwait, Israel, Denmark. The poor aren't hiding away at the edges, they're spread across the entire field of our vision. God, I hated some of their poverty. The cluttered, cramped place where deaf, blind Sophie has to live. The obscene hunger dogging Myles in his terminal illness. The fear of authority that made Sheila wince in her mothering. The shame of the Winter Works men in Newfoundland longing for steady jobs. The children living in parks. The dislocation that haunts Miss May's last days on this earth.

Ragged clothes, sickness, illiteracy, starchy food—these are the images we conjure when we think of the poor, when we think of our own smudged beginnings. No wonder we run from them, disown them, vow never to return. But my travels have taught me that these are only conditions, exteriors, the physical limitations of a people. It is poverty that is obscene, not poor people. They struggle mightily for grace and balance and are the essence of our nation's character. Could there be any better ambassador for Canada than Vera in Winnipeg, or Carl and Malcolm on Fogo Island?

I felt so good among them, authenticated by the instant welcome of Scouter in New Brunswick, Anne in Prince Edward Island, Gary and Jonene in Vancouver. I warmed myself with the love of poor fathers and mothers across the country, and was awed by their skill and common sense. I felt my own roots flower with their friendship and wisdom. I heard their stories and understood mine better.

But I'm not poor any more. I complete the circle of my history and cross back over the poverty line, watching my words and manners, moving into a stiffer self. What a different place middle-class life is—more self-conscious, cautious, mannered, coded. How insistently informed and expert we are over here, how little we speak from our hearts. I return to this good fortune more aware of my many debts.

My sense of the possible has been paid for by the people who came before: the ones who laid down the track, built the roads; who waited on tables, worked the mills, washed other people's floors. My own mother bore the wounds and went without so that I could have good food and warm clothes. The enormity of her gift only now finds words of gratitude. It is the poor who bought my future with their hard work and common citizenship. It's upon their backs that a richer Canada lifts itself.

The poor *are* getting poorer, of this I have no doubt. So are the middle class. One rainy night outside a Toronto concert hall, I see an Asian man with a sign on his back: "I'd rather work than beg." His wound is too obvious and passers-by pull into themselves. The man was laid off after nineteen years because the furniture plant he worked in moved south, and now he's run out of UI. In the silent exchange that is charity, we both know he might never work again. He is officially disappeared to that other Canada, and yet he stands so publicly on our sidewalk.

But how oblivious the rest of the country seems, obsessed with heaving itself into the twenty-first century. Hysteria over the national deficit creates terrible public stinginess. Canada's largest food bank can't get enough donations to feed the needy while a parliamentary committee decides to eradicate poverty by changing the way we define it. Headlines about welfare cheaters compete with grainy, black-and-white images of the poor as victims. The real details of their lives grow blurry in the fictions. Economic self-interest threatens to strangle all our hearts. We're told to hold fast, that we're at the dawn of a new global order. But who will this twenty-first century belong to?

Global restructuring means rootless capital, big money floating across borders. The people who move the money have no national allegiances, no sense of duty to a place, a community, the betterment of society. What do they care of Lionel, who prefers wandering the streets to the madhouse he calls home? These are not the paternalistic captains of industry who immortalized themselves with at least a few good deeds and favourite charities. There's no noblesse oblige here, no desire to comfort the widows like Libby or provide some dignity to the disabled like Sophie or allow Ghislain the full fruits of his labour. These new transnationals want profits. Their means are open, unregulated markets, cheap labour and a desperate, mobile work force. They need people like Ann to stir their toxic stews.

Governments the world over are bowing to the demands of these huge corporations, relinquishing precious sovereignty and national dreams, ceding control over environmental and social policies. National economies are being streamlined for the convenience and plunder of the transnationals. It's a kind of suicide, the pathetic attempts of an anorexic to achieve beauty by denying herself sustenance.

We're offering our most vulnerable citizens as human sacrifices to global restructuring, institutionalizing Third World poverty within what remains of our borders. Working people are being slapped back a generation, and the poor and unemployed cannot hope to ever move ahead. This isn't the dream my mother fed me on, nor the country she scraped and sacrificed to include me in.

Poverty is getting worse in Canada because there's no political will to stem it, because we insist on our social amnesia, because we're looking out for our own narrow interests. But a nation of poor people is a dangerous, menacing thing—just step on the sidewalks and see.

There is no lack of good and workable ideas about sharing fairly in the country's wealth. Many are election promises made and reneged on: a national day-care program, affordable housing initiatives, a real retraining effort, a decent minimum wage, a guaranteed annual income that could loosen welfare's chokehold on 2.5 million Canadians. But if the very notion of social justice is cut out of the national heart, if we perceive our national programs as an obstacle to economic progress (an unfair subsidy, an unfair tax, a financial drain); if the poor continue to be caricatured as parasites, then there is no place to begin again but at the beginning—in the stinking bog of social Darwinism. Is this our Canada in the twenty-first century? Is this the legacy we want to leave for our children?

My dear son, Liam, still wanders into people's souls with baby eyes. He doesn't notice shabby clothes or another child's lack of toys. He sees to the depths of character, as my own mother taught me to see. When we recently discussed *Jack and the Beanstalk*, I argued that Jack might be guilty of stealing the golden goose. "But Mommy," Liam said, "Jack's mommy dint got no money!"

With every ounce of my love I wish Liam a lifetime of meaning and prosperity. But one in three Canadians will be poor sometime in their lives; perhaps one day my son will be poor. It is all too possible, though I fear that for him less than an oblivious heart.

There but for the grace of God go all of us. The next century is yours, Liam. Take care of our country and the dreams of poor people. Work diligently for justice, appreciate what you've borrowed and remember that all of us share the commonest root. It is an inheritance to be proud of, not to be ignored. You come from poor people. We have built this country with the bare bones of our character. Never forget that.

NOTES

Research for this book came mostly from personal interviews with over 140 Canadians. Additional information was taken from a variety of government statistics and reports; especially valuable research and analysis was supplied by social policy and anti-poverty groups.

Among the sources I found particularly useful were:

Canada. Department of Justice. *Evaluation of the Divorce Act: Phase 2 —Monitoring and Evaluation.* 1988.

Canada. Employment and Immigration Canada. *Briefing Unit 1991-92.*

Canada. Health and Welfare Canada. *Health Status of Canadian Indians and Inuit.* 1990.

Canada. Secretary of State. *An Economic Profile of Persons with Disabilities in Canada.* 1990.

Canadian Council on Social Development. *Perceptions* 15 no. 3 (Summer 1991).

Clarke Institute. *Annual Report 1991-1992.* Toronto.

Investigative Productions. *Voices from the Shadows: The Welfare Poor Speak Out.* Documentary film. 1992.

National Anti-Poverty Organization. *Submission to the Standing Committee on External Affairs and International Trade on the North American Free Trade Agreement*. November 1992.

_____. *Written Submission to the Subcommittee on International Trade of the Standing Committee on External Affairs and International Trade*. November 25, 1992.

National Council of Welfare. *Poverty Profiles 1980-1990*. Autumn 1992.

_____. *Welfare Reform*. 1992.

National Voluntary Organization. *A Profile of the Canadian Volunteer*. 1987.

Newfoundland and Labrador. Department of Fisheries. *Changing Tides: A Consultative Document on the Fishery of the Future*. March 1993.

Dr. Don Offord. "The Ontario Health Study, 1983" in *Transitions*. Vanier Institute of the Family. June 1991.

David Ross and Richard Shillington. *Child Poverty and Poor Educational Attainment*, a report prepared by the Standing Senate Committee on Social Affairs, Science and Technology. May 1990.

Saskatchewan. Saskatchewan Agriculture and Food. *StatFacts*. August 1992.

Statistics Canada. *Agricultural Profile of Saskatchewan*. 1991.

_____. *The Daily*. April 28, 1992; October 13, 1992; April 27, 1993.

_____. *Labour Force Survey*. 1992.

_____. *Labour Market Activity Survey*. 1990.

_____. *Perspectives*. 1992.

_____. *Quality of Work in the Service Sector*. 1992.

Geoffrey York. *The Dispossessed: Life and Death in Native Canada.* Lester & Orpen Dennys, 1989.

United Nations Committee on the International Covenant on Economic, Social and Cultural Rights. *Consideration of Reports Submitted by States Parties under Articles 16 and 17 of the Covenant.* May 1993.

LINDALEE TRACEY is an award-winning journalist and writer for magazines and films. She writes extensively on public affairs, persistently exploring the social geography of Canada. Her articles have appeared in *Toronto Life, Canadian Living* and the *Globe and Mail Report on Business*. Her radio work includes feature documentaries for "Sunday Morning" and a stint as a producer for "As It Happens." She is the winner of several national magazine awards.

Lindalee Tracey lives in Toronto with her husband, filmmaker Peter Raymont, and their son, Liam. This is her first book.